"We should be doing this in a bed."

Alex's words were a caress as he gently pulled Erica down beside him on the living room floor.

"That's so passé. Anyone can do it in a bed." Erica gazed lovingly into his eyes. "I want you here. Now . . ."

"I want you, too, Erica. [illegible] won't hurt you? [illegible] feel comfortabl[illegible]

Erica would [illegible] looked so sin[illegible] rug burns?" she teased.

He tugged her r[illegible] open and swept his hands over her. "It's just that you're so incredibly soft. . . ."

"Mmm," she mumured as she pressed her lips against his shoulder. "So are you."

"Men aren't soft," he whispered. "They're hard."

Erica smiled devilishly as she trailed her hand slowly downward. "So they are. . . ."

Carin Rafferty adores children, but has never been blessed with any of her own. So Carin satisfies her mothering instincts by showering affection on her "baby" sister, her nieces, nephews and all her friends' children. She also tries to include children in her romance novels. *My Fair Baby* features a huggable little tyke, Joshua Stewart. So hang on to your hearts, ladies. Between baby Joshua and the gorgeous hero, Alex Harte, you're bound to fall in love!

Books by Carin Rafferty

HARLEQUIN TEMPTATION

281–I DO, AGAIN

HARLEQUIN AMERICAN ROMANCE

320–FULL CIRCLE
359–A CHANGE OF SEASONS

My Fair Baby

CARIN RAFFERTY

Harlequin Books

TORONTO • NEW YORK • LONDON
AMSTERDAM • PARIS • SYDNEY • HAMBURG
STOCKHOLM • ATHENS • TOKYO • MILAN

With love
to my sisters Chris Wilkerson and Connie Benson,
and their adorable "holy terrors,"
who keep me laughing.
How blessed you both are!

Published October 1990

ISBN 0-373-25419-9

Printed in U.S.A.

1

ALEX HARTE GASPED in disbelief when he stepped into Erica Stewart's garage. According to the woman who'd sent him in here to wait, this was Ms Stewart's studio. The walls were covered with paintings of evil monsters in every shape and size, and he turned in a slow circle in an attempt to take it all in. He finally decided that with the addition of some blackout curtains, eerie lighting and a few cobwebs, the woman could charge admission to the place as a house of horror.

He grimaced in distaste as he moved closer to one particularly gruesome painting with a placard that read Demons And Damnation. The demon hovering over the bloody carnage—indistinguishable as animal or human—was vile enough to make a grown man sleep with a night-light.

Alex shivered involuntarily and lowered his gaze to the newspaper article framed beneath it. The headline read, Monster Woman Strikes Again. The gist of the article was that the horrifying poster for the movie *Demons and Damnation* had helped make it a box-office hit. The reporter went on to say that Ms Stewart, whom the press had fondly dubbed Monster Woman, was fast becoming the most sought-after artist in her field, and horror fans could look forward to many more of her tantalizing creations on book covers and movie posters.

Tantalizing creations? Alex returned his attention to the painting and eyed it askance. He could think of a good number of words to describe it, and tantalizing wasn't even in the running.

He spun around, surprised by the low chuckle behind him. The woman leaning against the door frame flashed him a brilliant smile. Her short cap of light brown hair was a riot of unruly curls that framed an oval face. Her small freckled nose was wrinkled in amusement, and her dark brown eyes were dancing with undisguised laughter, which, Alex realized with chagrin, was directed at him. His discomfiting thoughts about the painting must have been reflected on his face.

He automatically dropped his gaze to her clinging yellow T-shirt with the words "Have You Scared Someone You Love Today?" printed across it in bold black letters, and then lower, to the pair of Daisy Mae denim cutoffs that revealed the best pair of legs he'd seen in ages.

He reluctantly tore his eyes away from those legs and a pair of slender bare feet with pink-tinted toenails when the woman said, "My cleaning lady should have warned you about the paintings. They are a bit startling."

"That's the best understatement I've heard in years," Alex said as he dubiously eyed a group of paintings on a nearby wall. He returned his gaze to her face and asked, "Does your cleaning lady scare ten years off all your visitors' lives, or is her sadistic streak reserved for pesky advertising executives?"

Erica arched an approving brow. She liked people who got right to the point, even if they were pesky advertising executives who refused to take no for an answer.

She stepped into the garage. "Actually, it's reserved for visitors who show up on my doorstep unannounced and uninvited."

She watched a gleam of amused challenge enter Alex's hazel eyes, and he nodded, as if acknowledging that she'd just thrown down the gauntlet. Then he smiled at her, and Erica gulped.

Until that moment he'd looked like any other successful businessman, albeit more handsome than most. With his professionally styled dark brown hair, charcoal-gray three-piece suit and glistening black wing tips, he could have stepped off the cover of *Gentlemen's Quarterly*.

But his smile dispelled the stuffy boardroom image. It was indisputably the sexiest, most rakish smile she'd ever seen in her life, and when his eyes slid down her in a slow, blatantly male appraisal, her stomach contracted in a totally feminine response.

The mesmerizing spell of his smile was shattered when he said, "Your son doesn't look anything like you."

The flame of anger that shot through Erica brought a rude retort to her lips, but she bit it back quickly, reminding herself that Mr. Alexander Harte wasn't the offender in this maddening situation. He was simply an innocent victim of her mother's fame-crazed machinations.

"Josh takes after his father. Look, Mr. Harte. . . ."

"Call me Alex."

Erica raked a hand through her hair in frustration when he treated her to another of his disarming smiles. "Fine. Look, Alex . . ."

"May I call you Erica?"

She scowled at him, aware that his interruptions were an attempt to throw her off balance. They only made her more determined to have her say and send him on his way.

"Yes. Now, about these commercials. As I told you on the phone—innumerable times," she added disapprovingly, "Josh isn't available. My mother took him to the audition without my permission, and I sincerely apologize for that. However, I have no intention of putting my son to work, and the sooner you accept that fact, the better off we'll both be."

Alex watched determination etch itself onto her delicate features and firm her wide, sculptured mouth into a resolute pout. But her resolve couldn't match his own.

It had taken Alex six months to find the perfect three-year-old boy to launch his advertising campaign for the My Fair Baby line of clothing. My Fair Baby was the largest and most lucrative client his firm, Harte Advertising, had landed to date, and a successful campaign would finally put him on top in the advertising world. He wasn't about to let the account slip through his fingers, and that was exactly why he'd decided to pay Erica Stewart a personal visit. He'd figured that if the lure of money wouldn't make her capitulate, his persuasive charm would.

But how did a man charm a woman who was nicknamed Monster Woman and painted terrifying demons for a living? Her macabre talent just didn't mesh with her lively, wholesome looks, and Alex had a feeling that that paradox was the key to what he wanted.

"I was wrong," he drawled softly, provocatively. "Josh has your delectable mouth."

Erica's jaw dropped and she stared at Alex in stunned disbelief. When he smiled at her again, she realized she was gaping and she snapped her mouth closed. But even grinding her teeth didn't stop the wave of sexual awareness that swept through her.

Good heavens, the man was the enemy! she railed inwardly. He exploited children. He wanted to capitalize on her son. And if he didn't stop smiling at her like that, she'd be groveling at his feet.

She peered at a painting over his shoulder, determining that it was an appropriate distraction. It was the first book cover she'd designed after she'd walked out on Mark two years ago. She'd secretly named the frothing monster *A Portrait of an Ex-Husband*. Just the thought of her stormy marriage was enough to put her back on even footing, especially when she recalled the child-custody battle Mark was now putting her through.

"Flattery will get you nowhere, Mr. Harte," she stated firmly as she glanced back up at his handsome face. "Josh isn't available for your commercials."

But Alex wasn't about to be thwarted. "Why not?"

"Because, at the inception of unions in this country they fought hard against child labor, and I'm a firm union supporter," she responded cheerfully, deciding that the best way to handle the man was to keep it light. "Would you like a glass of iced tea before you go?"

Alex quickly weighed his alternatives and decided that to leave would be a mistake. He also knew he had to get Erica Stewart out of her studio-garage. Intuition told him that the paintings gave her courage, and he couldn't ignore the shiver that crawled down his spine as he glanced around him. Once again he found himself wondering how a woman who reminded him of hot chocolate and homemade cookies could create nightmares.

"I'd love a glass of iced tea."

She nodded and walked away. Alex's gaze was glued to her slim figure as he followed her through the backyard and into the house. As he studied her slender back and watched her hips move in a natural, provocative sway, he decided that not only were her legs great, but the rest of the package was more than pleasing to the eye. He experienced a surge of spontaneous hormonal activity and let himself flow with the feeling, while wondering if he'd be able to use it to get what he wanted.

Erica's kitchen only emphasized her wholesomeness. It was white and yellow and big. A huge teddy bear cookie jar dominated the immaculate counters. A colorful needlepoint picture declared: There's No Place Like Home. A box of sugar-coated cereal sat on top of the refrigerator, and childish crayon drawings were anchored to every available spot on its door.

"Where's Joshua?" Alex asked as he pulled out a chair, sat down at the table and watched Erica retrieve a pitcher of iced tea from the depths of the appliance and pour it into glasses.

"At story hour at the library. Sugar and lemon?"

"Both."

She began to slice a lemon.

Alex wasn't aware that though outwardly Erica was the picture of serenity, inwardly she was fuming. She still couldn't believe her mother had taken Josh to the My Fair Baby audition, though she didn't know why she was surprised.

Erica had been a child model and had hated every minute of it. Her mother's ambition to make her daughter a famous personality had stolen away Erica's babyhood and childhood. Only when she'd hit the awkward stage of adolescence—all legs and arms and had no longer been "adorable"—had she finally been allowed to lead a normal life. Her mother had never forgiven her for the audacity of growing up, which had resulted in Erica living through turbulent and rebellious teenage years.

Now history was trying to repeat itself. Her mother was not only offering to handle Josh's career, but was accusing Erica of trying to exact revenge by denying her the happiness of reliving her halcyon days. Erica knew she was making the right choice for Josh, but her mother's accusations were still making her feel guilty. Was her mother right? Was Erica using Josh against her to exact revenge? She simply didn't have an answer, and she released an irritated sigh.

"Something wrong?" Alex asked when he heard the sigh.

Eric gave him a forced but breezy smile. "Of course not." She carried the glasses to the table and handed him one.

Settling into a chair across from him, she sipped the tea and regarded him. His bone-melting smile was gone, and he was peering down into his glass as though it were a crystal ball that would give him answers.

Suddenly his head shot up, and the intent look in his hazel eyes, which were more green than brown, made Erica squirm in her chair.

"My client is captivated by Joshua," he told her. "If I can't produce him, I'll probably lose the account."

If Erica had felt guilty before, she was now swamped with remorse. Exacting revenge on her mother was one thing. Dragging an innocent man into the middle of it was another. "I'm sorry."

One corner of his lips lifted in what could only be described as a half-grimace. "Not as sorry as I am. For the past five years I've been clawing my way to the top. It isn't easy to become a success in Los Angeles. Do you have any idea how many proven advertising firms I'm up against? Firms that have been in business longer than I've been alive?"

Erica shook her head, while mentally calculating his age. Somewhere between thirty-three and thirty-five, she finally decided. "You're young. You'll have another chance."

"No. If I blow this one, I might as well close up shop."

He set his glass on the table and stroked his immaculately groomed fingers against the condensation forming on its sides. The action was somehow erotic, and Erica found herself fighting against the urge to squirm again as she watched him.

She forced her eyes away from those stroking fingers and asked, "Don't you think you're being a bit melodramatic?"

"Not at all." Alex leaned back in his chair, stretched out his legs and crossed his ankles, looking far more relaxed in her kitchen than Erica would have liked. "I'm the new kid on the block, and I just landed one of the biggest advertising accounts to come along in a very long time. My competition is predicting that I'll fail, because they say I don't have the experience needed to handle an advertising campaign of this magnitude. If I lose the account I won't be able to convince another company of any consequence to take a chance on me. In the world of advertising, they live by the old adage, 'Once a loser, always a loser.'"

His smile returned, and this time it was even more devastating to Erica because of the vulnerability reflected in his eyes. With an inward curse, she leaped to her feet and walked to the kitchen sink. As she peered out the window over it, she decided that when she got her hands on her mother she'd shake her until her teeth rattled. If she hadn't taken Josh to the audition, Erica wouldn't be dealing with the aftermath.

Alex watched Erica as she tapped a fist against the edge of the kitchen sink. He could sense her inner turmoil and hoped it meant she was wavering. He knew he'd been taking a chance when he'd decided to tell her the unvarnished truth about the My Fair Baby account. He'd given her enough ammunition to take him to the financial cleaners if she agreed to a contract.

At this point, however, Alex was ready to mortgage his soul if need be. Success was so close he could taste it, and he was starving for it. He also realized that it was fast becoming a fading mirage when Erica turned back to face him, that damnable determination re-etched on her face and belying the regret shimmering in her big brown eyes.

"I'm sorry, Mr. Harte, but as sympathetic as I am with your situation, I have to think of my son. There is no way I'm going to let him be worked from sunrise to sunset."

Alex frowned. "Worked from sunrise to sunset? Where in the world did you get an idea like that?"

Erica's lips curved in response, but the action could in no way be described as a smile. "Once upon a time I was a child model, and I will not subject Josh to that type of life. It would be the same as selling him into slavery."

Alex narrowed his eyes and studied her assessingly. Her confession had just given him the answers to questions that had been deviling him about her refusal to negotiate a contract. But how should he respond? He'd heard the horror stories of child modeling from many an adult model, and though he knew that the industry had dramatically changed for the better during the past several years, he also knew that convincing Erica of that fact was going to be close to impossible. Old wounds didn't heal easily, and he was the perfect example of that fact.

In an effort to gain some time, he drained his glass and rose to his feet. He carried the glass to the refrigerator. Only when he reached it, did he look at Erica and ask, "May I help myself to another glass of tea?"

She nodded, her expression as wary as a cautious dog who was trying to decide if it faced friend or foe.

Alex turned his back on her and helped himself to the tea and lemon in the refrigerator. Then he retrieved the sugar bowl from the cupboard where he'd seen her store it.

After he doctored the drink, he turned and leaned casually against the counter, taking a sip of the tea while letting his gaze roam around the room.

"You know," he said after several minutes and as many sips had passed, "I envy your son. When I was a kid, I dreamed of living in a house with a big kitchen and a cookie jar full of homemade cookies. Unfortunately, my mother could barely afford the rent on our efficiency apartment, and her cooking skills were confined to cans and fast-food restaurants.

"Don't feel sorry for me," he added quickly as he transferred his gaze to Erica, who indeed had an expression of sympathy on her face. He gave her a beaming smile as he continued with, "I may have lacked homemade cookies, but I never lacked love. In fact, a smile and a hug from my mother was worth a thousand homemade cookies. It's just that..." His eyes moved away from her and again wandered around the room.

"It's just that what?" Erica prodded, drawn into his story, though she knew it was most likely a devious ploy. Her own childhood had been filled with the material, but it had lacked the emotional. She'd have been far more willing to forgive if she'd ever been convinced of her mother's love.

"I wish I hadn't been a reminder to her of all the things that might have been," he answered softly, almost absently. Then he shrugged, as if shedding the past.

Once again his eyes returned to her, and Erica felt herself captured by his compelling gaze. She wanted to reach out to him. To touch him. To communicate an understanding that she didn't really understand herself.

Instead, she linked her hands behind her back and asked, "What makes you so sure the cookie jar is filled with homemade cookies?"

"I just know. Just as I know that no matter what I say, you aren't going to listen to me, because you have a preconceived notion of what I am and what I do. Because of your own experiences you won't allow yourself to be open-minded about how I conduct my business. You've lumped me in with everyone from your past, and you've condemned me with them."

Erica opened her mouth to deny his words, but on second thought closed it. It was true. He represented everything from her past that she hated. He was a reminder of everyone who'd ever used her and abused her by housing her beneath hot, glaring lights for hours at a time. By making her pose in unnatural positions until her very bones ached. By scolding her when her hair became mussed, or when she'd yawned in boredom or exhaustion, instead of smiling.

"You're good, Mr. Harte," she stated ruefully. "For a minute there, you almost had me convinced that you're different."

"My name is Alex, and I am different," he said as he took a step toward her.

The manly scent of him filled Erica's nostrils and her fingers tightened around each other in response. He smiled again, and she hated him for the mush it created inside.

Josh. She said the name internally and firmly as she fought against the charisma of the man. Josh was all that mattered. It was bad enough that his father was using him to get back at her. It was bad enough that her mother was using him to relive a past that Erica had no desire to remember. She wasn't going to let Alexander Harte become one more hurdle she had to leap over. She simply wasn't going to do it!

But then he touched her. His fingers were cool from his ice-laden glass, which, oddly enough, made it seem as if they were scorching her heated cheek as they grazed over it. Her nerve endings hummed. Her body thrummed. Her throat closed with the overwhelming emotion of womanhood longing to burst into full bloom.

"Don't!" She jerked away from him awkwardly, almost falling, and then almost falling again when he reached out to steady her.

He dropped his hand to his side and gazed at her with a look of concern that was even more disconcerting.

"Are you all right?" he asked.

Erica nodded, although she was anything but all right. She was feeling angry and confused and betrayed. She turned away so he wouldn't see the tears in her eyes. She wasn't going to cry! Tears weren't going to solve her problems. They were only going to compound them, because tears were weak, and she could no longer afford to be weak. For Josh, she had to be strong. For Josh.

"Erica," Alex said quietly, insistently, "I'm not your enemy."

"Of course you are," she stated hoarsely. "You want to use my son, and I'm not going to let anyone use him. He's only three years old. He has a right to his childhood, and I'm going to make sure he exercises that right."

"I'd be disappointed if you didn't protect his childhood," Alex countered, moving another step closer to her but stopping abruptly when she stiffened. "But you have the wrong idea about my commercials. We've already started working with a three-year-old girl who will be

Joshua's counterpart. Our sessions are two hours a day, four days a week, and they're more like playtime activities than a job. I would never take a child and turn him into a workhorse. If you don't believe me, then call the girl's mother. She'll tell you exactly what we're doing."

"I don't care what you're doing," Erica said as she spun around to face him, determined to send him away. But he was so close that the order to leave froze in her throat. His look of vulnerability was back and it scrambled her thoughts as much as his closeness scrambled her insides.

"I have a copy of his audition tape in my car," Alex informed her. "Let me leave it with you. Look at it before you make any decisions."

"All right," Erica conceded, even though she had no intention of changing her mind. Acquiescence, however, would get the man out of her house, and considering the unsettling effect he was having on her, she couldn't get rid of him soon enough.

"Great. I'll be right back."

As Alex hurried out the back door, Erica drew in a deep breath, but it didn't alleviate the restless yearning stirring inside her. In fact, his absence intensified it, making her feel more alone and confused than ever.

She moved shakily across the room and collapsed in the kitchen chair she'd vacated earlier. How could a stranger make her feel so . . . alive?

She was still pondering the question when he returned, and Erica felt a new surge of guilt as she took note of the hopeful excitement radiating from him. He really believed that she was going to reconsider his offer, and she knew she should tell him otherwise. But if she did that, he'd most likely stay to argue with her, and she knew that would be dangerous, because if he stayed, he might actually convince her to change her mind.

Alex joined her at the table and studied her face as he placed the videotape and a piece of paper in front of her. Her expression was neutral, which worried him. If she was wavering, he didn't dare push too hard. However, if she was still adamantly opposed to her son doing the commercials, he couldn't walk away without another hard push. It was the first time in his career that Alex felt as if he were walking a tightrope without a safety net.

Cautiously he said, "I've written down Sharon Perkins's number. She's Susie's mother—the three-year-old girl I mentioned. Please call her. She can tell you how we deal with Susie, what the work schedule is like and anything else you want to know."

He paused, waiting for Erica to respond. When all she did was gaze down at the videotape and paper, he reached out and laid his hand over hers in an effort to gain her full attention.

Erica jumped at the contact that caused an exhilarating zinging sensation to course up her arm. Her first impulse was to snatch her hand away, but her self-protective instincts warned her that such an action would be far too revealing. She slowly raised her eyes to his face.

He gave her still another of his knee-buckling smiles as he said, "All I ask is that you talk to Sharon and look at the videotape. If you still feel the same way after you've done that, I promise I won't bother you again." He rose to his feet and said, "I'll call you in a few days."

Before Erica could respond, he walked out. As she listened to the door close behind him, she peered down at the paper with the neatly printed name and telephone number on it.

She wasn't going to change her mind, but she supposed it wouldn't hurt to make the call and look at the tape, especially since he'd promised that he'd finally leave her alone if she did so. And that was what she wanted, wasn't it?

She waited for that inner voice of conscience to give her a resounding, "Yes." When it remained silent, she gnawed on her bottom lip in consternation.

2

ERICA HUNG UP THE TELEPHONE with a disgruntled sigh. Sharon Perkins had not only confirmed Alex's claims about her daughter's working schedule and environment, but she'd nearly repeated it word for word. Knowing that Alex hadn't had time to call and instruct the woman on what to say, Erica decided that they must have set up their story ahead of time.

She couldn't blame him, she thought as she crossed to the television and flipped it on. While it warmed, she slipped the videotape he'd given her into the VCR. He'd made it quite clear that his business was on the line, and on that point at least, she'd believed him. But even though she understood his motivation, she couldn't help feeling disappointed by his duplicity.

"I go now, Señora Stewart," her cleaning lady, Rosita Sanchez, announced as she walked into the living room.

Erica smiled at the small, middle-aged Hispanic woman, whose services were the one luxury she'd afforded herself since the divorce.

Rosita was a quiet, reserved woman, a widow who had emigrated from Mexico twenty-five years before, bringing with her her three young daughters. During that quarter of a century, she'd raised those three girls alone and by the dint of hard work, overcoming everything from prejudice to a language barrier.

Erica knew that Rosita's efforts had paid off handsomely. One of her daughters had graduated from law school and was working as a public defender. Another had recently become a certified public accountant. The third had just been accepted into medical school.

Erica not only admired, but was in awe of Rosita. The woman emanated strength and pride. She also had an unbending streak of independence that Erica would give her eyeteeth to have.

Erica had had to bite her tongue to keep from laughing when, six months before, Rosita had arrived in a rage and informed Erica, "My daughters want me to quit working and let them take care of me. Hah! I will never take their money. When you take money, you owe. If you owe, they feel they have the right to tell you what to do. I work hard so I can do what I want to do."

"Perhaps your girls are only trying to pay you back for everything you've done for them," Erica had suggested.

Rosita had muttered what Erica suspected was a curse, but her knowledge of Spanish was too limited for her to tell for certain.

"They already pay me back by being successful," Rosita had stated staunchly. "Now they are grown, and I can live my own life. Maybe I will even remarry."

Rosita had done exactly that three months later, and Erica had been envying the continual blush of color that had lit Rosita's high cheekbones ever since. It was the blush of love.

"I'll get your money," Erica said as she walked across the room and retrieved her purse.

While she pulled out her wallet, Rosita said, "That Mr. Harte, he was *muy bueno*, no?"

Erica glanced up at Rosita in surprise. Though Rosita occasionally discussed her own personal life, she was far too discreet to ever comment on Erica's.

"Yes, he was *muy bueno*," Erica agreed reluctantly.

Rosita gave a sage nod. "It is good to have a handsome man around. It takes your mind off your problems."

Erica's responding chuckle was mirthless. "That may be true in some cases, Rosita. Unfortunately, this handsome man is one of my problems. He wants to pay me a great deal of money, and all I have to do in exchange for it is put Josh to work." When Rosita looked confused, Eric said, "He wants Josh to be in his television commercials."

Rosita's spout of Spanish was so rapid that Erica didn't understand one word of it. Then the older woman shook her graying head in resigned dismay and said forlornly, "It breaks a *madre*'s heart when her babies must sacrifice, but sometimes we have no choice. You need big money to fight Josh's *padre*, no?"

"Yes, I need big money to fight Josh's father," Erica again agreed reluctantly, knowing that Rosita would have had to be deaf not to have overheard Erica's many discussions—not to mention rantings and ravings—about the child-custody battle. "But I can't put Josh to work. He's just a little boy. It would be too much of a sacrifice."

Rosita's expression softened with understanding, and she reached out and patted Erica's arm in a solicitous gesture. "Sometimes a *madre* must make hard choices, but we must think of what will be the best for our babies as the years pass. If Josh must sacrifice now, will he not be rewarded with a lifetime with you?"

"I suppose so," Erica answered, her brow creased in thought. "I hadn't thought about it that way."

Rosita gave another sage nod. "A *madre*'s heart always leads her way, but sometimes she must say no to her heart and let her head lead." She slipped the money from Erica's fingers. "*Buenas tardes,* Señora Stewart."

"*Buenas tardes,* Rosita," Erica repeated by rote.

The ramifications of Rosita's words were bouncing through Erica's head as she put away her purse, walked to the VCR and pushed the Play button. Then she walked to the sofa, sat down and curled her feet beneath her.

It was early June and the weather was in the mid-seventies, but Erica shivered with a chill as she watched a series of numbers roll across the screen. Then the chill faded and was replaced with love as Josh's familiar face appeared. He was truly his father's son, Erica acknowledged without a twinge of rancor as, for the first time, she critically studied Josh.

He had Mark's sun-bleached blond hair, though he had inherited Erica's unruly curls. His face was round with youth, but showed the promise of a lean, aesthetic bone structure. His eyes were wide and blue and sinfully long-lashed. And, she realized with a pang, Alexander Harte was right. Josh had her wide, mobile mouth.

In another fifteen years, her son would be a lady-killer, she decided, and it wouldn't be just because of his looks. It would be because of the angelic devilry that danced in his eyes—because of his infectious laugh and contagious verve. Because of the innate loving nature that was so pure it made her heart ache.

But would those qualities remain if Mark won his custody suit and Josh was shuffled back and forth between his parents, never finding stability? Never able to depend on a steadfast environment?

She found it ironic that until she'd packed her bags and walked out when Josh was a year old, Mark had barely noticed his son existed. During the past two years, Mark had exercised his visitation rights exactly five times. Now he was claiming in his petition to the court that he missed his son desperately, and since he was moving to New York City, he wanted to have custody of Josh six months out of every year.

If Erica could have convinced herself that Mark was sincere, she might have been willing to give joint custody a try, but she knew that Mark didn't really care about his son. He was simply using Josh to strike back at Erica. To punish her for doing the inconceivable, which was walking out on him.

Tears welled into her eyes and she blinked them back desperately. When she'd married Mark, she'd been head over heels in love, but during the next four years love had died a piece at a time. In its place had come disgust and resentment and even pity, for in the end, she had felt sorry for her ex-husband, whose self-indulgent weaknesses had been inborn.

Mark didn't need to hold down a job and didn't even try to. He'd inherited enough money and power to carry him through a lifetime of sybaritic pleasure, and every day of his life revolved around self-gratification. For him, nothing was sacred. Not even his wedding vows.

At first, he'd kept his infidelities a secret from Erica, but by the time they'd celebrated their second anniversary, he'd begun to flaunt them. Erica, so damn insecure because of her own past, had blamed herself, and when she'd become pregnant by accident, she'd been certain that a child would be the magic cure.

Hope does spring eternal, she now thought wryly as she watched Josh, laughing in uproarish pleasure, prance across the screen. Mark hadn't even been at the hospital when she gave birth. In fact, the first time he'd seen his son was the day she and Josh had been released and sent home, and Mark had grumbled the entire time because he'd had to get up so early when he'd been up so late the night before.

The sound of a car horn interrupted her journey into the past, and Erica rushed to the door, smiling as she watched Josh climb out of her neighbor's car. He raced across the lawn and flung himself into her outstretched arms.

"How was story hour?" she asked as she hugged him close and wondered what it would be like if he was taken away from her. Hell. It would be hell.

"Fun!" he exclaimed. "There was a bear. His name was Win . . . Win . . ."

"Winnie the Pooh?" Erica guessed.

Josh nodded in excitement. "His friend was a big kitty!"

"Tigger," Erica provided.

"Uh-huh," Josh answered as he pulled away from her embrace. "Can I have a cookie?"

"Just one," Erica answered, closing the door as he ran into the house.

Josh stopped abruptly, his head tilted to the side as he stared at the television screen in absorbed fascination. "That's me!"

"It sure is," Erica answered as she walked to him and stroked his silken head. "Grandma took you there to play. Did you have fun?"

He tilted his head until it was horizontal to the floor. "Uh-huh."

Erica's throat closed over the next question, but she forced it out as she stared down into his beloved face. "Would you like to go back there to play?"

He shrugged in unconcern. "Uh-huh. Where's my cookie?"

"I don't have any idea," she teased. "Do you think we should check the cookie jar?"

Josh laughed and ran into the kitchen. Erica followed and smiled as she took off the lid of the cookie jar and lowered the ceramic container so Josh could help himself to his treat.

But as she watched him, her mind did the strangest thing. She didn't see a blond-haired Josh delving his pudgy hand into the cookie jar. She envisioned a dark-haired, sad-eyed, three-year-old Alex Harte.

"Ridiculous," she muttered to herself. "Absolutely ridiculous."

ALEX PACED through his office, ignoring the pile of telephone messages on his desk from clients. They were his bread-and-butter clients, and he'd be devoted to them for the rest of his life. But My Fair Baby was big-time. It could zoom him to the top and once he was there, no one would ever be able to bring him back down.

He flung his suit coat across the back of his desk chair, unbuttoned his vest and pulled the knot of his tie halfway down his chest. He opened the top two buttons of his silk shirt and sighed in relief as he took a deep breath, and then another.

"So close," he muttered to the empty room. "I'm so damn close."

Erica Stewart held his future in the palm of her small, feminine hand, and he couldn't see any way he could keep her from crushing it closed—from destroying every one of his hopes and dreams.

Survival struggled inside Alex. Survival so intense it hurt. But in its wake came acceptance, because he knew that if she turned him down, she'd be doing it out of love for her son, and he would accept that, for if there was one emotion Alex did understand, it was maternal love.

His mother had been a member of the gentry who'd been led astray by a very married and now famous political leader. When she'd become pregnant and refused to consider abortion or adoption, her family had disowned her. His father, who appeared almost daily on the national news, and frequently with his wife of forty-two years, had never seen his only son or even acknowledged his existence. It was funny, but Alex had no desire to see him, and it wasn't out of respite. It was simply out of an acceptance of who and what he was.

He was a bastard. It was a fact of life he'd had to face at the age of five when he'd come home bloody and beaten from his first day at school. His mother had cleansed his wounds silently. She'd held his head to her breast in comfort. She'd told him that the future was his to make, and that no one could take that future away from him. For her, he'd become what he was today, or at least, what he was trying to become.

He dropped down into the chair behind his desk and hit the remote control switch that turned on the VCR. He watched Joshua Stewart dance across the screen.

The boy's eyes were an impossible blue. His face was a Rubens fantasy of cherubic perfection. His laugh would tug at the heart strings of a Scrooge.

Alex slumped in his chair, rubbed his hands over his eyes, and glanced back up at the television screen. If he searched for another six months—or even six years—he'd never find a little boy as captivating as this one, and if he didn't produce him, he could kiss the My Fair Baby account goodbye.

Survival once again prodded at him, and he reached impulsively for the telephone as a sudden idea struck him.

"Hello?" Erica's voice was husky when she answered on the other end.

"Alex Harte here," Alex stated. "I know I said I'd give you a few days to think, but we're doing a commercial tomorrow with Susie Perkins. I thought you might like to come to the studio and see what we do and how we do it."

Erica drew in a fortifying breath and released it slowly. Alex's deep voice vibrated in her ear as Rosita's words resounded in her mind. Sometimes a mother had to lead with her head instead of her heart, and she did need the money to fight Mark. Good attorneys were expensive, and she couldn't afford not to hire the best.

"I'd like that."

"Great," Alex said, inwardly sighing with relief. "Four o'clock. Check with the guard at the security gate. He'll be expecting you. Do you need directions?"

"No." Erica's voice was filled with resignation. "I recognize the studio. I used to frequent it back in the good old days."

Alex's heart stilled momentarily and his hands became clammy. If the studio would be taking her on a stroll down memory lane, tomorrow could turn out to be a disaster. But it was too late to back out now. All he could do was hope that she'd be able to overlook the past and concentrate on the present.

"I'll see you tomorrow, Erica."

"Yes. Tomorrow." She hung up without even a goodbye.

ERICA HAD DECIDED that her best defense against the charms of Mr. Alexander Harte was a good offense, and she'd dressed carefully for her meeting with him.

Except for a light pink lip gloss, she'd foregone all makeup. She'd tortured her curly locks into as severe a hairdo as possible, though it was still far too carefree in her estimation. She'd countered her uncooperative tresses with a stark white, no-frills blouse and shapeless navy blue suit, colors that did absolutely nothing for her. Even the timelessly styled navy blue pumps on her feet were for effect, not comfort, and she'd wanted to free her pinched toes and run barefoot thirty seconds after she'd donned them.

One look in the mirror had convinced her that she was about as appealing as a prison matron. So why was Alex looking as if he could eat her up when he met her outside the studio entrance and helped her out of her car?

Alex bit the inside of his cheek to keep from laughing as his gaze flicked over Erica's outrageous outfit. She reminded him of Beulah North, a middle-aged spinster who'd lived two floors down from him as a child. On Beulah, the clothes would have resembled armor. On Erica, they positively incited a man's most primitive fantasies and his fingers itched to strip the clothes off her.

"Right on time," he stated in his most businesslike tone.

"I believe in punctuality," Erica stated, trying to mimic the formal inflection in his voice.

"Commendable," Alex answered, glancing away from her so she wouldn't see his twitching lips. "Ready to go inside?" he asked when he'd gained control over his mirth.

But he needn't have bothered to try to hide his hilarity. Erica's eyes had been glued on the ominous door the minute she'd stepped from the car. Memories were haunting her. Memories that made her nauseated and weak and terrified.

"Erica?" Alex murmured in concern as he searched her pale face.

Her head jerked up and she gave him a weak smile. "Of course I'm ready to go inside."

Alex, sensing her distress, took her elbow and gave it a reassuring squeeze as he led her through the door.

The commercial was in progress and Erica didn't need to be told that silence was necessary as Alex maneuvered them through a maze of wires and cameras.

They stopped outside the pool of light that highlighted the little girl commanding center stage, and Erica couldn't help her soft intake of breath as she gazed at the child.

Susie Perkins was as ethereal as Josh was hardy. Where Josh's blond curls hugged tightly to his head, her equally blond, but wispy, silken hair fanned around her fragile face. Her eyes were as clear a blue as Josh's, but they held a dreamy quality instead of mischief. Even her high, tinkling laughter was in counterpoint to Josh's deeper guffaws.

"What do you think?" Alex whispered in her ear.

Erica shook her head and whispered back, "Heavenly. She's absolutely heavenly."

Heavenly. Alex tested the word and decided it described Susie Perkins to a tee. He smiled as he watched the child grab a fluffy stuffed cat from the pile of toys surrounding her, and with a squeal of delight, rush to her mother to show her.

Erica stiffened as she watched the child run out of the pool of light. Her breath caught in anticipation of the roar of disapproval that would follow. Several seconds passed before she released it slowly and peered toward the director's chair in confusion.

The man hadn't uttered a word. He'd simply held his hand up, which Erica realized was a sign for the cameras to stop rolling. Several minutes passed before Sharon Perkins, who'd been oohing and aahing over the toy, led her daughter back to center stage where a woman met them and combed Susie's ruffled hair.

Then, after Sharon had coaxed Susie's attention back to the toy pile, she retreated into the shadows. The procedure repeated itself a dozen times during the next hour.

"Seen enough?" Alex finally asked.

Erica nodded and followed him outside. As he walked her to her car, Erica fought against a myriad of conflicting emotions. It appeared that Alex's director wasn't like the Simon Legrees she'd worked for as a child, but she couldn't help but wonder if the entire session had been staged for her benefit.

"Well?" Alex drawled expectantly as he leaned against her car, prohibiting her from climbing inside and racing away as she so desperately wanted to do.

"These commercials must be costing you a fortune," Erica said.

Alex gave a noncommittal shrug of his wide shoulders. "They'll hopefully make an even bigger fortune."

"At the rate Susie's going, it'll take you two weeks to film the one you're working on."

"We're looking for perfection, Erica, and perfection takes time."

He sounded so sincere, and Erica searched his face, looking for some sign of deceit, some element of fraud. Something—*anything*—to uphold her earlier protestations. All she found was that damnable hopeful expectancy that he'd displayed the day before.

"There must be times when the director and camera crew get frustrated," she offered half-heartedly.

Alex chuckled, and the sound sent a shimmer of pleasure rolling through Erica. "The camera crew gets paid by the hour. They're in favor of frustration. As for Ron...well, he may get frustrated at times, but he agrees with my concept on these commercials. We want them to be natural. We want the audience to see them and think of the special little girl or boy in their life and imagine what they'd look like all dolled up in My Fair Baby clothing.

"Since we're dealing with babies and not trained actors," he continued, "natural means a lot of hard work. If we have to sort through several hours of filming to splice together the perfect thirty- and sixty-second commercial spots, then that's what we'll do."

Erica nervously rubbed her hand against her thigh. She was running out of arguments. What she'd just seen inside wouldn't be detrimental to Josh, but the fact that she'd be using him for the almighty dollar still grated. It put her into the same greedy category as her mother, though her motivation was not for fame but to maintain her hold on her son. The distinction didn't help.

Finally it was time that gave her the perfect foil. "Isn't it awfully late in the day to work a child?"

Again, Alex gave her that noncommittal shrug. "Sharon chose a late-afternoon session. She says Susie is irritable in the mornings, and that her best time of the day is late afternoon and early evening. If you agree to let Josh do the commercials, you'll have the latitude to dictate his hours. After all, you know when he's at his best, and it would be ridiculous for us to try to work with him when he isn't at his best."

Erica had run out of objections. So what did she do from here? She needed to think everything through. She needed to weigh the good against the bed. She needed to come to grips with her own past.

Alex watched the emotions fly across Erica's face and a part of him urged that he reach out and pull her close to comfort her and reassure her. That urge startled him. Erica was nothing more than a pawn, he reminded himself. An attractive one, but a pawn nonetheless. She was the means to his success.

Alex glanced down at his watch. "It's after five. How would you like to join me for an early dinner?"

Erica gave a shake of her head. "I have to get home. Josh is at my neighbor's."

"So give her a call and tell her you're going to dinner. You've just entered into the realm of rush-hour traffic. Even if you left this very minute, you wouldn't make it home much sooner than you would if you left an hour from now."

Erica knew he spoke the truth, but time on the freeway was preferable to time in Alex's company. He looked too good. Smelled too good. Talked too good. And there was that darn smile of his that was coaxing her to say yes.

"I need some time to think," she told him.

Alex didn't need to ask her what that statement meant. He also knew he wanted to spend some time with her. Erica was the most uncomplicated—which, conversely, made her the most complicated—woman he'd met in years. She also fascinated him. She looked like a brunette Barbie doll, even in her ridiculous suit and blouse that would have made his fashion-conscious secretary choke on her morning croissant. She was the quintessential all-American, girl-next-door, who just happened to paint monsters for a living.

"I promise that we won't discuss the commercials. I hate to eat alone, and you'd be doing me a favor if you joined me," he cajoled.

If his smile had been coaxing before, it was now spellbinding. She said yes without even realizing it.

"Great," Alex said. "My car's this way, and . . ."

While he was speaking, he levered himself away from her car and the full impact of him suddenly slammed into Erica. She'd been aware of him all along, of course, but it had been on a subliminal level. Now just the thought of climbing into a car with him was enough to put every nerve in her body on red alert.

"I'd rather follow you in my car," she said. When he gave her a questioning look, she frantically searched her mind for a reasonable excuse. "Something might happen to Josh and I'd have to leave right away."

Alex started to tell her that the restaurant was only a few blocks away and he could deliver her back to her car in less than five minutes. However, if the look on her face hadn't stopped his words, the death grip she had on her purse did.

"Okay," Alex murmured, wondering what had sent her into a sudden panic. "I'll get my car and meet you here in a minute."

As he walked away, Erica climbed into her car and leaned her forehead against the steering wheel, fighting to gain control over the flash fire of desire raging through her. She managed to at least get herself down to a low burn, but she knew it wouldn't take much to reignite the flame.

"Dear Lord," she prayed, "if you aren't going to give me strength, then at least give me a sign that this, too, will pass."

Alex chose that moment to honk his horn and Erica rolled her eyes heavenward.

"If that was your idea of a joke," she muttered disgruntledly, "you definitely need to work on your punch line."

3

THE RESTAURANT WAS CALLED China House and was no bigger than a hole-in-the-wall. The interior, however, was pleasantly decorated in an appropriate Oriental theme, and the delicious aromas filling the air had Eric salivating the moment the door closed behind them.

It was apparent that Alex was a frequent patron. The Chinese waitress greeted him with a flirtatious warmth as she led them to a small, intimate table in the back of the room. She returned a moment later with menus and a pot of tea.

As Alex filled Erica's cup, he said, "I should have asked if you liked Chinese food, but if you don't, they also have a good selection of American dishes."

"Actually, I love Chinese food," Erica said as she lifted the cup and took a sip of the floral-scented tea. It was the only way she could keep from staring at the man, and he was certainly worth staring at. He'd been handsome in his gray suit yesterday, but he should be outlawed from wearing navy blue, the very color she was wearing in inglorious splendor. "Unfortunately, I haven't eaten it in years. My ex-husband hated it, and Josh's idea of a gourmet meal is hot dogs and macaroni and cheese."

"It sounds like Josh has the palate of a typical three-year-old," Alex responded as he tucked away the information on her ex-husband. Alex had known Erica was divorced, because he'd decided to get around her refusal to negotiate a contract by contacting Joshua's father. He'd quickly shelved that idea when her mother had informed him of Erica's marital status.

Erica chuckled. "Josh is the typical three-year-old, period."

Alex smiled as he watched her lean back in her chair, finally beginning to relax. "Aah," he drawled knowingly, "we must be referring to those horrible years infamously known to all mothers as *the tempestuous threes*."

Erica laughed aloud at the comically ominous inflection he'd applied to those last three words. "Boy, you hit that nail on the head. I love Josh dearly, but my favorite times of the day are naptime and bedtime." She frowned. "Good heavens, that makes me sound like an awful mother, doesn't it?"

"No," Alex answered, resisting the urge to reach across the table and brush away the frown lines. "It makes you sound like a normal one. My mother has always claimed that if nature was fair, a woman's feet would sprout roller skates during her children's toddler years."

Erica grinned at that. "Your mother sounds like a smart woman."

"Mmm, she is."

Erica watched in fascination as his eyes took on a warm, faraway glow, and she knew instinctively that his mind was lost in some loving memory of his mother. Would Josh feel that deeply about her when he was Alex's age? she wondered. She fervently hoped so.

"Does your mother live in L.A.?" she asked.

Alex shook his head. "She decided last year that she wanted to be footloose and fancy-free, so she bought herself a small motor home, joined a caravan of roving retired persons and headed across country. The last postcard I got was from Gettysburg, Pennsylvania. It said they'd be heading north for the summer, and then they'd go south for the winter."

Erica's mind began to work overtime as he talked. Yesterday, he'd said his mother had barely been able to pay the rent on their efficiency apartment when he was a child. Apparently her circumstances had changed dramatically over the years if she could not only afford a motor home, but constant traveling.

"Your mother's retired?" she questioned next.

Alex laughed. "Good heavens, no. She's only twenty-three years older than me. That would make her—" his forehead wrinkled as he did some mental arithmetic "—fifty-seven."

Erica did some quick mental calculations of her own. Alex was thirty-four, six years older than her. "But you just said that she joined a caravan of retired persons."

"Yes, but they hired her on as their entertainment and tour director."

"I see."

Erica took another sip of tea, feeling uncomfortable in the silence that invariably stretched between two virtual strangers after they'd exhausted a conversational topic. She searched her mind for something to say, but she'd never been very good at extemporizing, particularly in the company of a gorgeous man.

"Would you like to call your neighbor before we order?" Alex asked when he noticed the waitress approaching.

"Call my neighbor?" Erica repeated, confused by his question.

"Yes. You know, the one who's baby-sitting Joshua."

"Oh! Yes, of course," Erica murmured as she rose hastily from her chair, horrified that she hadn't thought about making the call herself. "I can't believe that I forgot. I need to let her know where I am, so that if she needs me, she can find me."

Good heavens! she groaned inwardly when Alex grinned. She was babbling on about the obvious. That was only one step above blathering about the weather, which she'd probably be reduced to doing next if she didn't find something else to do with her mouth.

"Since you've eaten here before, why don't you just order me something you think I'd like," she suggested.

"Sure," Alex agreed, indulging himself in a little ego stroking as he watched her hurry to the public telephone across the room. He was fairly certain that he was the first man to ever make her forget her son, and he wondered what else he could make her forget as he indulged himself in the fantasy of exploring her delectable lips.

He gave a deprecating shake of his head when his mind conjured up the image of a pliant Erica pressed against him from shoulder to knee as they shared a steamy kiss. Erica Stewart was definitely off-limits, because she was the kind of wholesome woman a man committed himself to. Alex had already made one journey down the road of connubial disaster. He had no intention of making another. He placed their order.

"Sorry it took me so long," Erica said breathlessly when she returned to the table. "Josh had to tell me about the new picture he's drawn, which was a roundabout pitch for a puppy. Laura, that's my neighbor, has a black Labrador retriever. Josh and Tina—that's Laura's little girl—torment the poor thing by treating him like a horse, and. . ."

Her voice trailed off when she glanced up and saw that Alex was grinning again. She blushed. "I'm sorry. You couldn't possibly be interested in all this."

"On the contrary. I'm very interested in dogs who pose as horses. If he's really good in portraying the role, I might be able to put him under contract. Dogs are house-trained. Horses aren't."

Erica laughed. "Do you always think in terms of business?"

"No," he said, wondering how he could get her to laugh again. It was such a delightful sound. Rich and throaty and wholly feminine. "I sometimes think in other terms."

Erica reached nervously for the teapot as his gaze roamed over her face and settled on her lips, making her throat go dry. If he was thinking in the terms she thought he was thinking in, she definitely needed to steer their conversation back toward business.

"About the My Fair Baby commercials..." she began.

"Stop right there," Alex commanded. "I promised that we wouldn't talk about the commercials, and we're not going to talk about them."

"But I wanted to ask..."

He reached across the table and placed a finger against her lips. "Not tonight, Erica. If you have questions, then call me tomorrow. I'm in the office by nine."

Erica could only nod in mute agreement, because before he'd pulled his finger away, he'd stroked it across her lower lip, sending a bolt of pleasure to the center of her womb.

If her legs would stop trembling uncontrollably, she'd jump to her feet and run for her life, because she knew in that moment that Alexander Harte could be as deadly to her as contracting a case of the Black Plague. She also had a deep suspicion that she'd have a better chance of recovering from the latter than the former.

Alex was having similar thoughts as he met Erica's startled, wide-eyed gaze. Soft. She looked so soft and touchable. And he wanted to touch her. Everywhere, in every way. He closed his eyes and smothered the low groan coming to life deep in his chest.

She wasn't the first woman who'd stirred him up like this, and he knew she wouldn't be the last. She was, however, the first one since his divorce who'd made him feel that he wouldn't be satisfied with just a good roll in the hay. That made her as dangerous as unstable nitroglycerin. Too bad he'd never mastered the knack of flirting with danger, which was why, in this age of life-threatening social diseases, his sex life just about qualified him for priesthood.

Thankfully, their food arrived, and Erica gaped at the numerous dishes the woman piled on the table.

"Expecting an army to join us?" she asked, her earlier unease instantly forgotten at the tantalizing aromas teasing her nose. Her stomach grumbled softly in approval.

Alex grinned. "Just a combat unit." He lifted a lid off one serving dish. "Beef with Chinese vegetables." He lifted off a second lid. "Chicken with black mushrooms. And, of course," he continued as he set the lids on the table and gestured grandly toward a large platter, "sweet-and-sour shrimp."

Erica eyed the dishes with ravenous delight before she glanced up at Alex with a mischievous smile. "What are you having?"

Alex laughed. "From the look on your face, crumbs."

"That sounds reasonable. I can spare a crumb or two," Erica said with a chuckle as she piled steamed rice on her plate and covered half with a portion of the beef and half with a portion of the chicken. After applying a sparse amount of soy sauce, she filled her fork and released a hum of pleasure as she put it in her mouth. "Sinful," she murmured a second later. "Absolutely, positively, mouth-wateringly sinful."

"Gosh, I'm disappointed," Alex teased. "I thought you said you loved Chinese food."

Erica gave an insouciant shrug and flicked her tongue across her lower lip to capture a piece of rice clinging to it. Alex's body went from hot to hotter to hottest at the provocative gesture, and he nearly broke the chopsticks in his hands.

"What can I say? I'm a master of understatement," she replied as she reached out and lifted a shrimp, dipping its crusty tempura coating into the sweet and sour sauce. She popped it into her mouth and closed her eyes in rapture as she chewed.

Alex exchanged his chopsticks for the more sturdy stainless-steel fork that lay beside his plate as he fought against the surge of desire that came to life at her expression. It was exactly how he envisioned her looking as she made love. Maybe it wouldn't be so bad to do a little flirting with danger, and self-imposed celibacy was becoming a bit wearing.

The next several minutes passed silently. Erica was so absorbed in her enjoyment of the meal that she barely spared Alex a glance. Alex, however, was unable to take his eyes off her and could have been munching on cardboard for all the attention he was paying to the food.

He knew that eating could be a sensuous act, but with Erica it was as titillating as erotica. In fact, there were a few times that she made it downright X-rated. Alex went through three glasses of ice water before finally asking for a pitcher of it.

Erica suddenly peered at him, looking as if she were waking from a satisfying dream. "I'm sorry," she said. "The food's so good that I've been ignoring you."

Alex had to clear his throat. "Your apology is unnecessary. I'm just glad you're enjoying your meal."

She nodded and smiled. It was a gentle, guileless smile that sent Alex's hormones on a disturbing rampage. He downed another glass of ice water.

"So tell me about yourself," she said.

"What would you like to know?" Alex asked.

"I don't know. How did you get into advertising?"

"By accident, actually," he answered. "I was a business major in college, and during my senior year I worked part-time for an ad agency. My title was gofer, but I used to sit in on all the staff meetings. I needed a good project for my marketing class, and I decided to come up with an advertising campaign for one of their prominent clients who was asking for something new and innovative."

"And your class project was exactly what the client wanted," Erica guessed.

"Exactly," Alex agreed. "The boss liked what I'd done and offered me a full-time job when I graduated."

"And as the old saying goes, the rest was history."

"Not quite, but it was a beginning. I discovered that I liked the business. It challenged me, gave me an outlet for my creativity, and it paid well."

Though he'd listed the pay on the last of his list, the emphasis he placed on it made Erica wonder if he shouldn't have mentioned it first.

"Money means a lot to you?"

Alex leaned back in his chair and stroked his chin thoughtfully. "Not the money specifically, but the success it equates with."

"In other words, you want to be somebody," Erica said, feeling somewhat disappointed.

"Don't you?"

"Not at all."

Alex's grin was as amused as it was disparaging when he murmured, "'Ms Stewart, whom the press has fondly dubbed Monster Woman, is fast becoming the most sought-after artist in her field, and horror fans can look forward to many more of her tantalizing creations on book covers and movie posters.'"

Erica blushed deeply at the quote from the framed newspaper article that hung below her most successful endeavor to date.

"Okay," she relented. "I have my share of egotism, but I'm not after fame and fortune. I'm simply doing what I do best, and thank heavens, it pays the bills."

"And the notoriety doesn't hurt."

"No, it doesn't hurt."

"Then we really aren't that different after all, are we?"

Denial leaped to Erica's lips, but she couldn't utter the words, because she didn't know how to make him see the difference. What she did was a means to an end, not an end to a means, and she knew instinctively that that was what Alex was after.

She absently sipped at her tea as she studied him. Physically, he was already superior. Why was it so important that he excel on the other end of the scale?

"I answered your questions," he said. "Now, it's your turn to answer mine. Why do you paint monsters for a living?"

Erica blinked in surprise at the question. "Why?"

"That's what I asked."

"Because I'm good at it."

He chuckled. "I never said you weren't, but it isn't exactly the most conventional way to make a living, especially for a woman."

"Your chauvinism is showing, Mr. Harte."

"It wouldn't be the first time, and I doubt it'll be the last," he answered easily. "And the name is Alex."

Alex. She could taste his name, and it was almost as delicious as the morsels she'd been stuffing into her mouth. "If I had to give a reason for my talent, I guess it would be that I've always loved to be scared. When I was a kid, I lived for Friday and Saturday nights when my mother would let me stay up to watch horror movies on the late show, and when I'm asked to come up with a monster vision, there are always plenty of people in my past to provide me with food for thought."

"What kind of people?"

"Just people," she said with a vague wave of her hand, not willing to go into the psychology behind her statement. Then she glanced at her watch. "It's getting late. By the time I get home, it'll be Josh's bedtime."

"Fine. I'll have the waitress pack up the leftovers for you."

"Don't be ridiculous. You keep them."

"I'm not being ridiculous. The only thing I hate more than eating alone is eating leftovers alone."

"It sounds lonely."

"It is lonely."

Erica glanced down at her hands. How could she possibly reply to that? To her immense relief, the waitress arrived and carried away the remaining food.

Alex busied himself with the bill. Erica busied herself by retrieving her purse. The waitress returned with three good-sized containers. Alex gathered them all as he rose to his feet.

"I'll walk you to your car," he said.

Erica didn't bother to remind him that she was parked in the space next to his own car.

When she unlocked and opened her door, Alex handed her the cartons. She settled them into the passenger seat and turned back to him, saying, "Thanks for dinner. I enjoyed it."

"Me, too. We'll have to do it again."

Erica's stomach fluttered in anticipation of seeing him again, and her mind scolded her severely. The man was interested in her son, not her. It was just as well. Josh kept her running, and when she wasn't busy with him, she was trying to meet her deadlines. She didn't have time for a man in her life right now. Still, tonight had been nice. She would enjoy doing it again.

"I'll call you in a few days about the commercials," he told her.

All the good feelings from the evening evaporated. "Yes, about the commercials."

She started to climb into her car when Alex said, "Erica?"

"Yes?" she responded as she straightened and turned toward him.

"I'm going to hate myself for this," he said huskily.

"Hate yourself for what?"

"This."

Before her mind even had a chance to register what was happening, she found herself in his arms.

His lips skimmed across hers so lightly that she was certain she'd imagined it. But then they returned, hot and urgent and entreating.

She groaned at the conflict of emotions that surged through her. One part of her insisted that she pull away. Another part demanded that she surrender. But choices became inconsequential as his tongue laved across her lower lip and then demanded entrance into her mouth.

She groaned again as her arms wound instinctively around his neck. He responded with an urgent moan as his hands grasped her hips and melded her against the cradle of his thighs.

His stirring desire made her own senses implode. She couldn't get close enough to him, and her hands left his neck to burrow beneath his suit coat. She stroked his wide chest with one and caressed his taut buttocks with the other. Heaven help her, she'd missed this closeness with a man. No, she'd pined for it. Yearned for it. Even sat down and cried for it. She simply wasn't the kind of woman meant to traipse through life alone. She was a woman who needed a significant other, which was why she'd fought so hard for her doomed marriage long after any sensible woman would have accepted the inevitable.

"Oh, God," Alex said in a strangled whisper as he pulled her closer.

"If that's a prayer, I agree," she murmured throatily. "If it's a curse . . ."

"If it's a curse, what?" he gasped as he peeled his lips away after another heart-stopping kiss.

"I agree."

Her words relieved the tension—reminded him of where they were. He sighed and rested his cheek against her impossibly silken hair.

"I wasn't going to kiss you."

She leaned her head back so she could look at him. "Then why did you?"

His lips twitched. "A man can only ignore so much bribery."

"Bribery! I didn't bribe you."

"All right, seduction."

"I didn't do that, either!"

He tugged gently on the lapel of her suit jacket. "Of course you did. This outfit alone has been driving me to distraction."

"But I look like a frump," she announced with a confused frown.

"And frumpish becomes you. So does Chinese food. The way you eat it nearly sent me over the edge. I kept imagining your lips and tongue moving over me the same way, closing over me the same way, and . . ."

"And," Erica interrupted as she took a shaky step backward, his words far too erotic to listen to any longer, "I need to get home."

Alex released her reluctantly when she took still another step backward. "I'm sorry, Erica. I didn't mean to offend you."

"You didn't," she said. "It's just that . . ."

"It's just that what?" he encouraged when she didn't continue.

"Did you kiss me because you wanted to, or because you're after Josh?" she asked baldly.

The only sign of Alex's instant rise to temper was a twitch of muscle along his jaw. He could feel it leaping, pulsing. "What do *you* think?" he bit out.

"I think I've made you mad," she said with a wry little smile. "But if you're honest with yourself, you won't blame me for asking. It always behooves a woman to define where she stands."

Alex stuffed his hands into his pants pockets and stared up at the smoggy sky overhead, deciding that he didn't like daylight savings time. By now, it should be dark, which would provide him with a protective cover as he sorted his way through her question. Instead, he'd be doing so in full view of her searching, probing eyes.

He hadn't consciously kissed her because he was after her son, he finally decided, but there was a nagging part of him that said he could have done so subconsciously. He was attracted to Erica, but he'd been attracted to other women and had managed to ignore his masculine urges.

He returned his eyes to her face. "I don't know," he responded honestly.

Erica repressed the feeling of disappointment welling up inside her. At least he'd been truthful, but to her chagrin, she almost wished he'd lied.

"Good night, Alex," she said as she slipped into her car, turned the ignition and drove away.

Alex scowled after her, feeling angry, confused and, quite bluntly, horny as hell.

"Dammit, I kissed you because I wanted to!" he exclaimed in a low, furious voice.

Unfortunately, the revelation had come too late. Now, he'd not only screwed up his chances of getting his hands on Joshua Stewart, but he'd blown any chance he'd had of getting to know the boy's mother.

"MAMA, LOOK AT MY PICTURE!" Josh exclaimed, and Erica stepped away from her easel to peer down at Josh's miniature easel that stood beside hers.

"That's absolutely the most beautiful picture I've ever seen," she told him as she eyed the watercolor squiggles he'd smeared on a small canvas.

Josh tilted his head back and grinned at her, and Erica chuckled. As usual, he had more watercolor on him than on the canvas, and if he had any true artistic talent, it was still latent. But he enjoyed the activity, and Erica was determined to encourage him in any endeavor he attempted, something her own mother had never done with her. Her mother's philosophy had always been that if it wasn't an activity guaranteed to make money, it wasn't worth pursuing, and she scoffed at anything as frivolous as a hobby. Erica found it ironic that her mother's obsession with fame and fortune had nearly destroyed her parent's marriage, and yet it was the few sound investments Erica's father had made before his death that kept Madelaine Harris off the breadline.

It was almost as if thoughts of her mother had conjured her up, because at that moment, Madelaine appeared in the doorway.

"Good heavens, Erica, this house of horror is no place for a small child!"

"Grandma!" Josh yelled and rushed toward the older woman.

Erica smiled ruefully as she watched her mother deftly accept Josh's kiss while managing to keep his paint-stained hands and clothes away from her designer-label dress.

"Joshua Stewart, you are a mess," Madelaine proclaimed. "I stopped by to see if you want to go shopping with me, but if you do, you're going to have to get cleaned up."

"I'll give Josh a bath," Rosita announced as she magically appeared at Madelaine's side.

"Rosita, you don't have to do that," Erica immediately objected. "I don't pay you to bathe Josh."

The housekeeper smiled as she took Josh's hand. "I don't mind. Also, the mailman is at the door. He has a certified letter for you."

When the housekeeper and Josh had disappeared, Madelaine walked into the garage and glanced around her surroundings in disdain. "You spoil the help, Erica.

As you said, you pay her, so her job is to do whatever you ask her to do."

"Rosita is my housekeeper, not a nanny, Mother. It isn't her responsibility to bathe Josh," Erica said as she headed for the door.

Madelaine gave a dismissive shrug. "I'll wait for you here. If it's a certified letter, it's bad news."

Erica soon discovered that her mother was right. The letter was from Mark's attorney. Everything in Erica rebelled at opening the envelope in front of her mother, but curiosity and a good dollop of fear had her ripping it open the instant she returned to the garage.

At first, her mind refused to accept what she was reading, but when she read the letter again and skimmed over the attached legal documents, she had to sit on her stool to keep from collapsing.

"How bad is it?" Madelaine asked.

Erica handed her mother the documents, too close to tears to speak.

Madelaine perused the material and then shook her head. "I told you you were foolish to leave Mark. I knew something like this would happen."

Erica's temper erupted, and she welcomed the anger because it took the edge off the terror curled in her stomach. "Mark was sleeping with anything in a skirt!"

"That may be true, but you were married to him and had access to his bank account."

"There is more to life than money, Mother."

"Like what?" Madelaine snapped.

"Like pride," Erica shot back.

Madelaine waved the papers at her. "And this is exactly what your pride has gotten you. Mark is suing for full custody of Josh because he's remarrying and can provide him with a set of parents. My word, Erica, the man has money pouring out of his ears and can give Josh anything he wants, including a purportedly loving stepmother. What have you got to take into court to counter all of that?"

"Love," Erica answered.

"Yeah," Madelaine muttered. "That and a quarter won't even buy you a cup of coffee. What are you going to do?"

"Fight him."

"That takes money. Where are you going to get it?"

"I don't know," Erica confessed. She released a bitter laugh. "You know, I never thought I'd say this, but you were right. I never should have signed that damn prenuptial agreement when I married Mark."

"Well, you should have at least negotiated on it," Madelaine said as she strolled around the room, eyeing the paintings hanging on the wall. She shuddered in disgust and turned back to face her daughter. "But that's in the past, and nothing is going to change it. You have to worry about today, and the only way I can see for you to get the money to fight Mark is to let Josh do the My Fair Baby commercials."

Erica drew in a deep breath and released it slowly, because her mother's words suddenly brought an image of Alex Harte to mind. Along with the image, came the memory of their shared kiss, and she shook her head to dispel it.

It was evident that her mother took the gesture as a denial to her suggestion, because she said, "Erica, don't let your anger with me override your common sense. You need a lot of money and you need it fast. If you don't get it, you're going to lose Josh. That's one hell of a price to pay in order to exact your revenge against me."

"I'm not trying to exact revenge against you," Erica said with a weary sigh, tired of the argument her mother had been badgering her with for weeks.

"Can you look me in the eye and say that?"

Erica gazed at her mother, prepared to do exactly that, but the words wouldn't come. Instead, she found herself looking at her mother closely for the first time in years. She was shocked to discover that the eternally youthful Madelaine Harris was letting her dark brown hair go gray and was doing nothing to hide the fine lines of encroaching age on her face—a face that held a close resemblance to the one that Erica saw in the mirror every morning when she climbed out of bed. Was this what she'd look like twenty years from now?

She found the thought both startling and reassuring, for even though her mother was aging, she was doing it gracefully.

"I'm only trying to do what is best for Josh," she finally said.

"Then I know you'll do the right thing," Madelaine stated as she walked toward the door. "I'd better see if Josh is ready to go. I'll have him home in time for dinner."

Erica gave a resigned shake of her head when her mother left. She'd arrived without a hello and left without a goodbye. It was par for the course, but Erica had never gotten used to it. Just as she'd never really gotten used to her mother's obvious devotion to Josh. It made her wonder if their relationship would have been different if she'd been a son rather than a daughter.

But her lack of rapport with her mother was the least of her worries, she reminded herself as she rose off the stool and walked to the table where her mother had dropped Mark's latest bombshell.

As she once again reviewed the papers, she couldn't decide which she found more unbelievable—the fact that Mark had been able to dupe some other unsuspecting fool into marriage, or that he'd had the audacity to file for full custody.

She also admitted that her mother was right. She needed money and she needed it fast. The obvious solution was the My Fair Baby commercials, but what would she do if she signed a contract and then discovered that Josh hated the work? She'd either have to give the money back or force Josh to do them, which meant she'd be caught in a catch-22 situation.

What she needed was a compromise, but even if she could come up with one, would Alex Harte be amenable to compromise? They hadn't exactly parted on the best of terms at the restaurant. In fact, he'd looked pretty angry when she'd confronted him about his motivation for that kiss, and she hadn't heard a word from him in nearly a week. He'd probably changed his mind about Josh doing the commercials.

But Erica quickly dismissed that assertion, deciding that the man might be nursing a bruised ego, but he'd told her that without Josh he'd probably lose the My Fair Baby account. He'd call eventually, and when he did, she'd be ready for him.

4

ALEX STOOD BEHIND the camera lights and shook his head in amazement as he watched Susie Perkins romp around the stage in My Fair Baby playclothes. He knew that today's session was one of the best to date. He also knew that this was her last commercial, which meant he was going to have to break down and call Erica Stewart.

His mind instinctively balked at the suggestion, just as it had been balking whenever he'd reached for the telephone during the past week. The most maddening part of the situation was that he hadn't avoided making the call because he feared she'd say no, but because his desire to see her again was becoming greater than the desire to have her son in his commercials.

She's a pawn, he told himself for at least the hundredth time since she'd driven away from the restaurant. *Nothing more than a pawn.*

But every time he quoted those words, the feel of her in his arms came back to haunt him.

Soft. She was so wonderfully soft and pliable. She didn't rest against him; she melted against him. Her lips didn't kiss his, but clung to his. And she baked homemade cookies, for pity's sake!

His mouth watered at the reminder.

He stood up straight, locking his knees, but they trembled anyway as the image of Erica Stewart eating Chinese food teased at his mind. He refused to acknowledge what the memory did to the remainder of his anatomy. She wasn't some femme fatale. She was cute—no, make that adorable—and she had a three-year-old son and an ex-husband to contend with. No man in his right mind would take on that load!

But she was so damn soft.

"Cut!" Ron yelled, breaking into Alex's inner turmoil, and he knew that, ready or not, his hand had just been called. In another day—two at the most—Susie Perkins would be done. If Josh Stewart didn't start work within the week, he could kiss the My Fair Baby account and his career goodbye.

ERICA WAS SITTING on the sofa, her feet curled beneath her and her sketchpad braced against her thigh. She was so intent on getting the monstrous image in her mind down on paper that she jumped in surprise when the doorbell rang.

"I'm going to have to get one of those No Soliciting signs," she muttered as she set her sketchpad on the coffee table and rose to her feet. "And an answering machine," she added when the telephone began to ring.

She glanced between the phone and the door and decided it was first come, first served. But the moment she opened the door, she forgot about the ringing telephone, because Alex Harte was standing in front of her, bigger than life and more gorgeous than ever. She decided she was beginning to develop a fetish for three-piece suits, as her eyes automatically flicked over him.

"Your phone's ringing," he said, treating her to one of his toe curling smiles.

That wasn't all that was ringing, Erica thought when his eyes slid down her in a blatant appraisal that made her nerve endings begin to chime. She resisted the urge to tug on the hem of her shorts when his gaze landed on her bare legs and stayed, and she turned away from him, making a mad dash for the telephone.

She tried to tell herself that her breathless "Hello" was due to that dash, but she knew it was an outright lie. She was also chagrined to realize that she had one of those maddening computer messages on the other end, which meant she wouldn't have the opportunity to pull herself together before facing Alex again.

She dropped the receiver back into place and turned, only to discover that he'd entered the room and was holding her sketchpad.

He glanced up at her. "Did they hang up?"

"No. It was one of those crazy computer messages that tries to sell you something. I don't know why businesses use them. Everyone I know hangs up on them."

"You'd be surprised by how many people don't hang up. They really are a good merchandising tool. That's why I recommended it to several of my clients. Is this for a book cover?" he asked as he glanced back down at the sketch she'd been working on when he'd arrived.

"Yes."

"It's . . . interesting," he said, while thinking "bizarre" would be a better description. He wondered if she had trouble sleeping at night after spending the day creating monsters.

The thought spurred his fertile imagination into action, and he envisioned Erica tossing and turning among her bedcovers. But before he could evoke an image of just what he'd do to her to calm her, she asked, "What are you doing here?"

He dropped the sketchpad on the coffee table and grinned. "Would you believe I was just in the neighborhood and decided to drop in?"

"Sure. And the next thing I know, you'll be telling me that you shop at discount stores," she said, returning his grin.

"Actually, I do shop at discount stores," he told her as he tossed back the ends of his suit coat and stuffed his hands into his pants pockets. It was the only way he could keep from crossing the room and dragging her into his arms. He should have called instead of coming over, he decided as his eyes wandered down to her bare legs on their own accord. He wondered if they felt as silken as they looked. "They have great bargains. Where's Josh?"

Erica knew it was crazy, but she had a sudden urge to lie and say Josh was in his room. Some instinct for self-preservation was telling her it was dangerous to let the man know they were alone in the house. She also decided that she was going to have to make a major wardrobe change. Shorts might be comfortable, but the way Alex was looking at her legs made her feel positively naked.

"He went shopping with my mother. I expect them any minute."

Alex dragged his gaze away from her legs. "I kissed you because I wanted to, Erica, not because I was after Joshua."

Erica gulped as panic began to flutter in her stomach. What was she supposed to say to that? *Gosh, that's nice*? Or, *Thanks*? Or, *Let's do it again*?

"Would you like some iced tea?" she asked, taking a nervous step backward at that last traitorous thought.

He chuckled. "Sure."

Erica whirled around and made a hasty retreat into the kitchen. She jerked open the freezer door and welcomed the cold blast of air that hit her flushed face. *Alex Harte had kissed her because he wanted to!*

Of course he could be lying, the sensible part of her nature reminded as she grabbed a tray of ice cubes and closed the door. After all, he needed Josh for his commercials and would most likely say anything to get what he wanted.

She supposed she could test him by telling him she wasn't going to let Josh do the commercials, but what would she actually be gaining from the lie? Well, a half lie anyway, because she had come up with a compromise to offer Alex that wasn't exactly what he wanted, but suited her needs.

By the time she finished filling the glasses and doctoring Alex's tea with sugar and lemon, she'd come to the conclusion that all she'd gain by testing the man would be a good ego stroking, and even though she could use one, she wasn't frantic enough to resort to lying to get it. Besides, if *he* was lying, she'd end up getting a good ego bruising, something she definitely didn't need.

He was standing in front of a collage of family pictures when she returned to the living room.

"You have quite a rogue's gallery here," he said as he accepted the glass of tea she handed him. "It must be nice to have a big family."

"I'm an only child, so my immediate family is very small. Most of those pictures are of aunts and uncles and cousins. How big is your family?"

Alex shrugged. "To tell the truth, I have no idea. Like you, I'm an only child, but I was born out of wedlock. My father has never acknowledged me, and when my mother refused to consider abortion or adoption, her family disowned her. I've never met any of them."

"That's awful!" Erica said, appalled by the story. She'd often considered her mother a wicked witch, but she had to give credit where credit was due. Madelaine would have never disowned her under such circumstances.

Alex chuckled again. "Don't look so horrified, Erica. According to my mother, I'm lucky not to have met my rogue's gallery."

"But don't you ever wonder about them?"

"I did when I was a kid, but I don't anymore." He took a sip of tea before asking, "Have you reached a decision about the commercials?"

Erica regarded him curiously. He'd told the story about his birth so dispassionately that she truly believed that he wasn't disturbed by it, yet she'd seen a flash of something in his eyes before he asked about the commercials. It hadn't been pain, but more like a poignant sadness.

Suddenly she recalled that first day when he'd stood in her kitchen talking about his mother. What was it he'd said? Something like, *I wish I hadn't been a reminder to her of all the things that might have been.* She'd thought the statement odd at the time, but now she thought she understood it. She also wondered at what age Alex had decided to shoulder the blame for his mother's choices.

Compassion welled up inside her, and it took every ounce of her self-control to keep from reaching out to him. Intuition told her that to touch him would result in more than she was willing to bargain for. Kissing Alex Harte because he was sexy was one thing; kissing him as the result of a strong emotion was quite another.

"I have reached a decision about the commercials, although I think you'd call it more of a compromise," she said in answer to his question.

Alex inched a brow upward and regarded her warily. "A compromise?"

Erica nodded and walked to the sofa. She sat down and curled her feet beneath her before she said, "I'm still not convinced that Josh will like the work, so I've decided to go to contract on one commercial. If he does well on that commercial and appears to be happy, then I'll go to contract on the other three."

Alex took another sip of tea as he mulled over Erica's "compromise." It wasn't the type of contract he wanted, but he was desperate, and desperate situations called for desperate measures. By going along with her, he could at least give My Fair Baby one commercial to kick off their campaign, and it would give him time to look for a replacement if Erica wouldn't go to contract on the other three commercials. It would also give him time to work on Erica so he wouldn't have to look for a replacement.

And working on her certainly wouldn't be a hardship, he decided as he glanced at her. The hardship would be maintaining the distinction between "working" on her and seducing her, because she looked so inviting curled up in the corner of her overstuffed sofa that he wanted to do nothing more than cross the room and ravish her right where she sat.

He put a tight rein on his libido while silently chanting the litany of reasons why he couldn't get involved with her. She was the type of woman who would expect a commitment. She had a three-year-old son and an ex-husband.

And she had the best legs in town, he decided, his gaze once again drawn to them as she stretched them out on the sofa. Long, silken legs that would curl around a man and . . .

He downed the remainder of his tea, and still had to clear his throat when he said, "All right, Erica. We'll go to contract on one commercial. Would Josh be able to begin next week?"

Erica blinked at him in disbelief. "That's it? All right? We'll go to contract on one commercial?"

Alex chuckled. "What did you expect from me? An argument?"

"Well, I did expect at least a token argument," she admitted. "After all, I'm not giving you what you want."

"On the contrary. You gave me a yes, which is exactly what I want. Now all I have to do is prove to you that you've made the right choice."

Erica gazed at him suspiciously. "I'm serious, Alex. I'll only go to contract on one commercial, and I'm not open to negotiation."

"Who's trying to negotiate?" he asked with a wide-eyed, innocent look that Erica didn't buy for one second. "Will Josh be able to go to work next week?"

"He has a doctor's appointment on Monday, and I have an appointment on Tuesday that I can't miss, but I suppose he could go to work on Wednesday."

Alex nodded. "Wednesday it is. I'm going to be at the studio tomorrow morning. Why don't you bring Josh by? You can set up a shooting schedule with Ron and arrange for a fitting for Josh. It will also give Josh a chance to meet the people he'll be working with, as well as become accustomed to the studio. That way he won't be frightened by the new environment when he begins working."

Erica was touched by his seemingly sincere concern about Josh becoming familiar with the studio. "That's a very kind offer, Alex. Would ten tomorrow be all right?"

"Ten will be fine." He glanced at his watch. "I need to get back to the office. I'll have my secretary draw up a contract, and you can sign it tomorrow."

Erica rose up off the sofa and walked to him. As she accepted his empty glass, she shifted uncomfortably from one foot to the other. "We haven't discussed the financial arrangements."

Warning bells went off inside Alex, and he narrowed his eyes as he watched a crimson blush flood her cheeks. He'd known last week that he'd given her enough ammunition to take him to the financial cleaners, and it appeared that she was getting ready to use it. He braced himself for the bad news.

To his surprise, however, she didn't try to blast him. All she said was, "I only expect a fourth of the money, of course, but would it be possible to get the check tomorrow?"

So, she was doing it for the money. Alex found that realization startling, because up to this point she'd snubbed the money. He knew at that moment that if Erica hadn't needed it, she would have never let Josh do the commercial. What in the world had happened that would make her go against all of her principles and put her son to work?

Alex told himself it was none of his business. He told himself not to challenge fate. Whatever her problem was had proven to be his godsend, and he couldn't afford to screw it up.

She was staring down at her feet as she waited for his answer, and Alex hooked a finger beneath her chin and raised her head before he even knew what he was doing.

"What's wrong, Erica?"

He'd asked the question so softly and looked so concerned, that tears stung Erica's eyes. She blinked against the mist and resisted the urge to throw herself into his arms and tell him the whole sordid story about Mark and the child-custody battle. It would be so wonderful to share the load with someone who'd be solicitous and understanding.

But even if Alex would give her the support she needed, he was still a stranger. All she and Josh were to him was a meal ticket, and it was a pretty sad state of affairs when a woman had to share her troubles with a man whose total involvement with her was for his own pecuniary reasons.

"Nothing's wrong," she replied, forcing herself to give him a bright smile. "I'd just like to get paid when I sign the contract."

Alex knew she was lying, but he decided not to push. They'd be in constant contact during the next few weeks. He'd find a way to worm the truth out of her, and he was going to discover the truth, because the other three commercials could hinge on whatever was going on.

"I'll bring your check to the studio tomorrow."

"Thanks. I really appreciate it."

Alex left, and when he was gone, Erica leaned against the door and let out a sigh of relief. Then she rushed to her purse, pulled out her pocket calculator and divided the figure that Alex had quoted on the commercials by four. She'd been hesitant to do so before, because she'd feared that he'd insist on lowering the amount if he was guaranteed only one commercial.

As the figure popped up on the display panel, she discovered that it wasn't as much money as she'd hoped for, but it was enough for her to retain the attorney that she was meeting next Tuesday.

"Watch out, Mark, because the war has just begun," she stated in triumph as she stuffed the calculator back into her purse.

AS ALEX PACED OUTSIDE the studio, he decided that even though he was only thirty-four years old, he had to be going through mid-life crisis. All he'd been able to think about since he'd climbed out of bed this morning was the fact that he would be seeing Erica at ten, and he glanced at his watch to confirm what he already knew. Erica was twenty minutes late.

He told himself that she'd probably been delayed by the infamous Los Angeles traffic, which was murderous at its best. Twenty minutes wasn't anything to sweat about. But he was sweating. What if she had changed her mind about letting Josh do the commercial?

Alex stopped his pacing and drew in a deep, calming breath. He was noted for his cool logic and it was time to use it. If Erica had changed her mind, she would have called him. She wasn't the type of woman to leave a man hanging, and even if she was, they'd made a verbal contract. If she tried to renege on it, he'd show up on her doorstep and . . .

And what? Threaten her with a lawsuit? Hell, no. He'd show up on her doorstep and kiss her until she couldn't breathe.

So much for cool logic.

He resumed his pacing, chanting over and over that Erica was nothing more than a pawn. An attractive one, but a pawn nonetheless. She and her son were the key to his success. He'd finally be able to make all his mother's sacrifices worthwhile. He'd finally be able to make his ex-boss eat his disparaging words that had predicated failure. And most of all, he'd finally get his revenge against his ex-wife.

Just the thought of Kristen was enough to put him into a foul mood, and he was scowling when Erica pulled her car to a stop in front of him. The sight of her harried face and tousled hair through the windshield sent a white-hot bolt of desire flashing through him, and his mood darkened even further. Why was it that just the mere sight of the woman sent him over the edge?

"I'm sorry I'm late," Erica said when she climbed out of her car and warily regarded Alex's scowling countenance. "There was an accident on the freeway and I got off at the nearest exit. Unfortunately, so did everyone else. Traffic was bumper-to-bumper through the city, and..."

And why am I apologizing? she asked herself. One of her major problems with both Mark and her mother had been this terrible urge to always defend herself, and if she'd learned nothing else from nearly four years of counseling, it had been that it was ridiculous to apologize for events that were beyond her control. If Alex couldn't understand what had happened, then tough.

Since Alex still hadn't spoken, she ignored him, opened the back door of the car and began to release Josh from his car seat.

"Do you need any help?" Alex suddenly asked from directly behind her, and Erica's spine did a writhing snake dance at the sound of his husky baritone.

She swallowed hard, but her voice still cracked when she said, "No. We have the routine down pat."

She took more care than usual helping Josh out of the car, because she needed a moment to pull herself together. Good heavens, what was wrong with her? The man had been glaring at her when she'd arrived, but all he'd had to do was speak to turn her into soft butter.

By the time she closed the car door, she'd convinced herself that she was ready to face him. But when she turned and met his smile in full bloom, she knew she was doomed. The only way she'd ever be able to immunize herself against Alexander Harte would be if he was wearing a sack over his head.

"Hi," he said.

"Hi, yourself," she replied, nervously reaching down to stroke Josh's hair. "You remember Josh, don't you?"

"Of course," Alex said as he glanced down at the boy. "It's nice to meet you again, Joshua."

Josh was standing behind his mother, one arm clenched around her shapely linen-clad leg while he peered around it at Alex. Alex felt a stirring of déjà vu. He couldn't have been much older than Josh when the event had taken place, and he was surprised at how clear the memory was. He didn't remember who the man was that his mother had introduced him to, but he did recall why he'd liked him.

He reached into his pocket and snagged a coin. Then he squatted down so he was at Josh's eye level. Josh immediately ducked his head behind his mother, but curiosity got the better of him, and in just a few seconds, he peered around her again.

The moment he did, Alex reached out and pulled the coin from behind the boy's ear, saying, "My word, Joshua, you had a quarter in your ear!"

Josh grabbed his ear and burst into giggles. "Did not," he told Alex.

"Well, if you didn't, then I guess this quarter belongs to me." Alex began to pocket the coin.

"It's mine!" Josh exclaimed as he made a grab for the coin, and Alex laughed as he handed it to him.

"Maybe you should give it to your mother for safekeeping. Then when you get home you can put it in your piggy bank," he suggested.

But Josh gave a firm shake of his head and shoved the coin into his pocket.

Alex glanced up at Erica, his eyes dancing with devilry. "It looks as if he doesn't trust you."

"Oh, it has nothing to do with trust," Erica said, regarding her son in motherly amusement. "He's at that mimicking stage, and my next-door neighbor's husband carries his change in his pocket. Whatever Bob does, Josh does. Just about every pair of pants he owns has a hole in the pocket, but I suppose I shouldn't complain. Every little boy needs a male role model. Thankfully, Bob doesn't mind playing the role."

Alex would have had to be deaf not to hear the underlying bitterness in Erica's voice, and he mulled over her words as he rose to his feet. If her neighbor was acting as Josh's role model, where was the boy's father?

He didn't voice the question, however, because the less he knew about Erica, the better off he'd be. Instead, he extended his hand and said to Josh, "Would you like to come in and meet my friends? I know they really want to meet you."

Josh, who'd resumed his choke-hold on his mother's leg, hesitated for a moment, but then he suddenly released her and accepted Alex's hand. As Alex curled his fingers around the boy's tiny appendage and Josh gave him a shy smile, his chest went tight.

He'd always loved kids and had, as a young man, envisioned himself with a half dozen of them in tow. But children equated with mother, mother equated with marriage and marriage equated with divorce. He'd learned the latter from bitter experience, and he'd be eternally grateful that Kristen hadn't wanted a family. He wouldn't have been able to bear being a weekend father.

Alex gave an internal shake of his head to rid himself of the painful reminders of the past and led Josh inside.

Erica had been prepared to dislike each and every one of the people involved in the My Fair Baby commercials, but it was impossible to dislike people who appeared to be so genuinely interested in Josh. The cameraman lifted him up to the cameras and let him peer through them. The wardrobe and makeup staff made such a fuss over him that he was positively preening beneath their attention. The director, Ron Holiday, produced a virtual mountain of toys and sat in the middle of the floor to play with him.

"You're very lucky, Erica," Alex said when he joined her on the sidelines. "Josh is one of the most delightful kids I've ever met."

Erica gave him a wry smile. "Tell me that after you've seen him throw a temper tantrum."

Alex laughed. "He can't be that bad."

"That's what people probably said about Attila the Hun before they made his acquaintance." She glanced toward Josh, smiling fondly. "He has a temper. Thankfully, it doesn't erupt very often."

Alex sat on a nearby stool, bracing one foot on the floor and hooking the other on a rung. "I still can't believe he's that bad, but I do know it's difficult raising a child."

Erica returned her attention to him and chuckled. "It's not difficult, Alex. It's terrifying. When I was pregnant, I read every child-rearing book on the market. I thought I had parenthood down pat, but by the time Josh was a month old, he'd already destroyed that notion. He's stubborn and independent, and when he decides he's going to do something, nothing short of a freight train is going to stop him."

"Is this one of those confessions of, 'If I'd known what I was getting into I would have had second thoughts?'" Alex teased.

Erica's gaze wandered back to her son and she shook her head. "No. I'm glad Josh is stubborn and independent. Those are traits that denote strength. I just hope I succeed in channeling them in the right direction so that he's able to make them work for him instead of against him."

She gave Alex an apologetic smile. "I'm sorry. Here I am boring you again. Since Josh is occupied, now would be a good time for us to sign that contract."

Once again, Alex found himself deviled by questions about the mysterious Erica Stewart, because he had a feeling that she'd just revealed some very intimate part of herself. The problem was, he couldn't decide what part or what it meant.

"I wasn't bored, and the contract is in Ron's office."

Alex rose to his feet and took her arm. He led her through the maze of equipment and down a short, dark hallway, where he opened a door, flipped on the light and gestured her inside.

When she entered Ron's office, Erica decided that she'd seen larger closets. The room didn't have a window, and it was barely big enough to accommodate the desk, chair and two-drawer file cabinet crammed into it. She knew that since the studio was generally rented out on a short-term basis, the owners didn't feel obliged to spend money on office accoutrements. They poured it all into the latest camera equipment.

"It looks as if the studio still employs the local dungeon decorator," she stated dryly.

Alex chuckled as he closed the door. "Their accommodations are a bit sparse."

"Grim would be a better description," Erica said as she took note of the dingy walls, the bare light bulb overhead and the cobwebs in all four corners of the ceiling. "I should loan Ron some of my paintings. They'd fit right in."

"I'll tell him you made the offer, but don't expect him to leap at it."

"Why, Alex, I'm crushed," she said, her eyes dancing with laughter. "If I didn't know better, I'd think you didn't like my work."

"Don't take it personally. I don't like Picasso, either," he quipped.

"What have you got against monsters?"

He leaned a hip against the desk and crossed his arm over his chest. She shivered as his gaze drifted over her, giving her the feeling that he knew every detail about her, even the flaws that were camouflaged by her clothing.

"I don't have anything against monsters," he eventually said. "I wouldn't have a nightmare without them."

"You think I'm crazy, don't you?"

Alex shrugged as he studied her face. She looked so animated—so cheerleaderish that he almost expected her to pull out pom-poms and burst into a rousing cheer. "Let's just say that you don't look like a person who'd create monsters for a living."

"What should I look like?"

He shrugged again. "I don't know. I suppose you should have scraggly black hair, black beady eyes and a mole on the end of your nose."

Erica laughed in delight.

"You have one of the sexiest laughs I've ever heard," he said huskily as he reached out and ran the back of his fingers down her cheek. "You also feel as soft as velvet. That's what I remember most about our kiss, and it's been driving me crazy. I keep wondering if you're that soft everywhere."

Erica met his hazel eyes and was mesmerized by them. They were greener today, reflecting the color of his light green shirt. They were also charged with the chemistry stirring between them. The chemistry that she'd been purposely ignoring and had every intention of continuing to ignore. Alexander Harte made a career out of creating illusions. She couldn't help but feel that it was an illusion he was creating here when he murmured, "Are you that soft everywhere?"

Erica moved back a step and nervously crossed her arms over her chest. She'd never suffered from claustrophobia, but suddenly the walls of the room seemed to be closing in on her.

"Where's that contract?" she asked briskly, deciding that the best part of valor would be to ignore his question.

"Why are you refusing to acknowledge what's happening between us?"

She raked a hand through her hair, unaware that the resulting tangle of curls made her look more approachable—more desirable. She decided that she not only had to acknowledge what was happening between them, but had to put a stop to it—the sooner the better.

"Look, Alex, I will readily admit that I find you attractive. But I'm a mother with a three-year-old terror on my hands. Josh and I come as a packaged deal, and you just don't strike me as a man who is into the family setting."

"We could have an affair," he suggested.

Erica closed her eyes and shook her head. "I'm not the affair type, and even if I was, I have to consider Josh. He needs a steady influence in his life, and a man who comes and goes on the urging of his libido just doesn't fit the bill. Considering your past, you of all people, should understand what I'm saying."

"You really know how to kick a man where it hurts the most," Alex stated gruffly.

Erica opened her eyes, her expression conciliatory. "I wasn't trying to hurt you, Alex. I was only stating the truth."

For a moment, he looked as if he'd disagree with her, but he finally said, "Yeah. Well, we'd better get this contract signed."

ALEX KNEW THAT EVERY WORD Erica had spoken in Ron's office was the unadulterated truth, but they still grated. Her assessment of him made him feel shallow, and that irked him.

When Erica said, "It's time for Josh and me to go," Alex knew that he wasn't ready to let her go.

He swung Josh up into his arms. "I'm in the mood for an ice-cream cone. Why don't you and Josh join me?"

The refusal on Erica's lips was quelled when Josh yelled, "Yeah! Ice cream!" He wrapped his small, sturdy arms around Alex's neck and announced. "I want chocolate. And strawberry."

"Chocolate *or* strawberry," Erica corrected as she smiled at her son's bright face. It was his look of excited anticipation that made her decide to take Alex up on his offer. After all, what possible harm could come from eating an ice-cream cone with the man? "It's too close to lunch for you to have both."

Josh's face immediately screwed up in a mutinous pout at her words. When Erica's expression settled into one of determination in response, Alex knew that a temper tantrum was only a heartbeat away. He decided to diffuse the situation, because he was sure that if Josh misbehaved, Erica would stick him in the car and go home.

"I'll tell you what, Josh," he said. "You order chocolate, I'll order strawberry and we'll share. That way we can have both flavors without ruining our lunch."

Josh continued to pout as he considered Alex's suggestion, but he finally smiled and said, "Okay."

Alex winked at Erica. "Compromise is my middle name."

"It's called outright bribery," Erica muttered. "But you got him to agree to share, so I'll let it pass this time. He's going through a selfish stage and sharing is a dirty word, so make sure you make him live up to his part of the bargain."

"Don't worry," Alex said as he headed for the door . "I'm a closet chocoholic, so I'll make sure I get in my share of licks. The ice-cream place is only a block away. Do you mind walking?"

"Walking's fine," Erica replied as he opened the door for her. "Besides, Josh hates his car seat and getting him into it is a major undertaking. We could probably walk the block a dozen times by the time we got him buckled up."

"Another stage?" Alex asked as he settled the boy firmly on his hip.

Erica glanced up at him, and the humorous look in his eyes made her grin. "Exactly."

"Just how many stages is he going through?"

"Too many to keep track of," Erica replied, giving her son a mock-ferocious look. "You're a holy terror, aren't you, Josh?"

"Yeah," the boy agreed with a giggle. He rested his head on Alex's shoulder. "But you love me anyway."

"I sure do," Erica said as she reached out and tickled his stomach, making him giggle again.

Alex experienced a flood of mixed emotions as he watched mother and son interact. A part of them was a poignant reminder of the special relationship he'd had with his own mother as a child, but another part was that old, hungry yearning to be a part of a family—the yearning that he thought he'd laid to rest years ago.

But when Josh began to play with the knot in his tie, Alex was forced to acknowledge he'd never laid it to rest. He'd merely buried it so deeply that he'd been able to ignore it. Thankfully, they arrived at the ice-cream parlor a few minutes later, and he wasn't forced to analyze his discovery.

He sat Josh down on the high counter and looped an arm securely around the toddler so that any sudden move wouldn't send him tumbling to the floor. Then he turned his attention to the boy's mother.

"So, what's your pleasure, Erica?"

"Vanilla," she answered.

"Vanilla?" he repeated in comical disbelief. "My word, woman, they have nearly fifty flavors of ice cream, and you want vanilla?"

Erica shot him a disgruntled look. "I like vanilla."

He grinned. "So do I, but I can buy vanilla at the grocery store. Come on, Erica, live dangerously and choose something totally outrageous."

"I'm a mother, and mothers don't live dangerously," she replied, lifting her chin a determined notch.

"You're also a woman, and a woman owes it to herself to live dangerously every once in a while."

Erica gulped as his gaze once again traveled down her in the wake of his words. By the time he returned his eyes to her face, he'd proven his point. Not one inch of her felt motherly at that moment.

"How about strawberry shortcake?" he suggested in a husky croon that made her skin ripple with pleasure. "That shouldn't be too dangerous."

Erica had to clear her throat. "They only serve ice cream here."

"It's a flavor of ice cream. Number seventy-six on the menu, and I'll personally vouch for it."

After casting a quick glance at the menu to confirm his words, Erica said, "I, uh, guess strawberry shortcake would be okay."

"Great."

Alex gave the clerk their order. When it was filled, he handed Josh his chocolate cone, and Erica carried the other two to the one empty table in the room. Since it would only seat two people, Alex settled Josh on his lap.

Erica handed him his cone and gave a hesitant lick of hers before saying, "You were right. This is good."

"I'm glad you like it," Alex replied, wondering how he could sound so calm while watching Erica swirl her tongue around the ice cream. He decided that eating with the woman should be declared hazardous to a man's health, and he shifted Josh into a more comfortable position on his knee when her tongue made another foray into the confection.

He was so intent on watching Erica consume her cone that he was caught off guard when Josh suddenly declared, "I want strawberry!" and made a grab for Alex's cone. Both ice creams ended up in Alex's lap.

"Josh!" Erica yelped in horror as she watched ice cream tumble onto Alex's suit—a suit that had probably cost him as much as one of her mortgage payments! Josh promptly burst into tears.

"It's all right," Alex said, trying to remove the ice cream with one hand and calm the sobbing boy with the other. "It was time to take this suit to the cleaners anyway."

"But he's probably ruined it!" Erica said as she leaped to her feet, grabbed a handful of napkins and rounded the table to help Alex deal with the mess. When she reached him, however, she froze, because Josh's disaster had ended up in a very intimate area of Alex's lap.

Alex eased the napkins from Erica's grip. "Why don't you calm Josh while I take care of this mess? And don't worry about the suit, Erica. I'm sure the cleaners can handle it."

"I hope so," she mumbled as she hauled her son off Alex's lap and hugged him. "It's all right, Josh. It was just an accident, but you have to learn to ask for things instead of grabbing for them, okay?"

"Okay." Josh sniffed as he swiped at his eyes with balled up fists.

"Good. Now, tell Mr. Harte you're sorry."

He gave Alex a woeful look. "I'm sorry."

"It's okay, Josh," Alex said. "I know it was an accident."

"I'll pay the cleaning bill," Erica said.

"Don't be ridiculous, Erica. I told you that it was time for this suit to be cleaned."

"And I know a polite disclaimer when I hear one, Alex. I want to pay the bill."

Alex started to refuse her offer again, but he glanced up at her before he spoke. She had the same determined look on her face that she'd had when telling Josh that he could only have one flavor of ice cream. His gaze traveled from her to her son, who was watching him through huge, tear-washed blue eyes. They were everything he'd vowed to avoid, but he discovered that he didn't want to avoid them.

He told himself that it was only good business sense to get to know them. He needed to gain Erica's trust so that she'd go through with the remainder of the commercials, and the best way to do that was to spend some time with her so she could see that he was a sincere, upstanding businessman, not the ogre she perceived him to be.

But even as he offered himself the excuse, Alex admitted that that was all it was—an excuse to give him permission to do what he wanted to do, which was become intimately involved with Erica Stewart.

"I'll make you a deal," he said. "I'll pay the cleaning bill, and you can invite me to dinner tonight."

"All we're having is meat loaf," Erica automatically responded, too stunned by his suggestion to come up with any answer but the truth.

"I happen to love meat loaf." He dug a handful of bills out of his pocket and laid them on the table. Then he flashed her one of his devastating smiles. "Now, give me Josh and go get us another ice-cream cone. I'd get them myself, but I'm not exactly presentable."

Every self-protective instinct Erica had told her to tighten her hold around her son and run for her life. But her legs refused to listen as Alex gazed at her steadily while holding out his arms for Josh.

He was anathema, she told herself. He was representative of everything from her childhood that was miserable. He was only being nice to her and Josh because he needed Josh to do his commercials—because his entire goal in life was to make money hand over fist so that he could be somebody. She'd lived through that obsession with her mother, and she'd be certifiably insane to get within even shouting distance of him.

But he was the only man since her divorce who'd made her feel womanly and desirable. Would it be so wrong to flow with those feelings as long as she never lost sight of just who and what he was?

"We eat at six," she heard herself saying as she handed over her son, deciding that if the word fool had to be known by another name, it would be Erica Stewart.

However, Erica was tired of running scared. The man was merely asking for an invitation to dinner. She was an adult. She could control events. If things got out of hand, she could always ask him to leave. "Is that too early for you?"

"Six is fine," he said as he settled the boy on his knee and gave him a reassuring hug.

Then he began to develop his excuses to his secretary for leaving early when she'd followed him to the elevator this morning ranting and raving about the contracts that he needed to review and the correspondence that had to be signed. Josh and Erica had to be first priority. If they weren't, then his secretary couldn't expect a bonus come Christmas. In fact, if the My Fair Baby account fell through, she might not even be able to expect a job.

5

"JOSH, GIVE TINA BACK that block right now," Erica ordered when she saw her son snatch the block out of the little girl's hand.

"But it's mine!" he declared as he hugged the toy to his chest and glared at his mother.

"Well, it won't be yours for long if you don't give it back to Tina, because I will throw it in the trash," Erica threatened.

"I won't let you," he stated in defiance.

Erica, who was up to her wrists in meat loaf makings, gritted her teeth and said, "Joshua, if I have to come over there and take that block away from you, you are going to be one very sorry little boy. Now give Tina the block this instant."

Josh continued to glare at her, his mouth set stubbornly, but he must have realized that his mother meant business, because he finally handed Tina the block.

"I don't like you," he told Erica.

"Well, that's just tough because I love you anyway," she replied by rote as she shot her neighbor, Laura Halsey, a long-suffering look. "I can't believe he's become so selfish. He was never like this before. In fact, he used to want to give away his toys."

Laura chuckled. "It's just a stage, Erica. All my kids have gone through it. He'll outgrow it."

"Well, I hope he outgrows it soon, because the more he defies me, the more I begin to believe in corporal punishment."

Laura nodded in understanding. "I know exactly what you're saying, but it's been my experience that outside of the element of surprise they get with the first sound smack to their bottom, spanking isn't effective with a kid like Josh. You'll probably get better results if you just follow through with your threat and throw the toy away."

"At the rate he's going, that could wipe out his entire toy chest in one day," Erica muttered.

"Cheer up. It really does get better," Laura said as she walked to the refrigerator and helped herself to a diet soda. "Now, tell me about the man who's coming to dinner. I want to know every nitty, gritty detail."

Erica cast a censorious look at the grinning redhead. "There is nothing to tell. Josh dropped his ice cream on Alex's suit, and this is just my way of making amends."

"Sure. And Patrick Swayze called me this morning and asked me to have a wild affair with him," Laura stated airily. "I told him it would have to wait until April, because it would take me that long to lose these miserable twenty pounds. He argued of course, but I held my ground. Somehow Patrick Swayze becoming intimately acquainted with my love handles just doesn't sit well in my mind."

Erica chuckled and shook her head. "You're incorrigible."

"That's exactly what Patrick said. Now stop avoiding the issue and tell me about Alex Harte."

"I'm serious, Laura. There's nothing to tell," Erica said as she dumped the hamburger mixture into a roasting pan and began to mold it. "The man is gorgeous, and he kisses like a million bucks, but he isn't my type."

"You kissed him?" Laura yelped as she swooped down on Erica.

"Laura!" Erica scolded lowly. "The peanut gallery, remember?"

Laura shot a quick look in the direction of Tina and Josh. "They're so absorbed that they wouldn't hear an air raid siren. Besides, we aren't talking about the *biggie*." She returned her attention to Erica and lowered her voice to a conspiratorial whisper. "When did you kiss him?"

"I didn't kiss him. He kissed me," Erica replied begrudgingly as she dumped a can of tomatoes over the meat loaf. "But it didn't mean anything. It just happened."

"What are you saying? A kiss is just a kiss? Come on, Erica, that excuse didn't even work for Bogart."

Erica gave her friend a scolding look. "You watch too many old movies."

"You should watch more of them," Laura countered. "Kisses don't just happen, Erica. Not to people our age, anyway. We aren't exactly teenagers."

"We aren't exactly ancient, either," she stated dryly.

"Speak for yourself," Laura muttered. "I'm on the verge of thirty-five."

"I'll throw you an 'over-the-hill' birthday party," Erica said, her lips twitching.

"You do, and I'll kill you. That's not a threat, Erica. That's a promise."

"I'll keep that in mind."

Laura picked up a potato and began to peel it. When it was done, she rinsed it, cut it in half and dropped it into Erica's pot, saying, "Be honest with me, Erica. It wasn't just a kiss, was it?"

"No," Erica admitted as she raised confused eyes to her friend's face. "I haven't felt this way about a man since...

I've never felt this way about a man, not even Mark. I took one look at Alex, and it was lust at first sight." Her gaze wandered to her son, and then back to Laura. "But I have to think about Josh. Every person I let into my life, I'll also be letting into his. I know he's only three, but some of my earliest memories are ones that took place when I was his age. If I give into my baser instincts, I could be setting up a chain reaction that would affect him for the rest of his life."

Laura frowned as she began to peel another potato. "I wish I could offer some advice, but the truth is, I'm one of those lucky women who found the man of her dreams at an early age and he's never lost his luster." She chuckled. "Well, that's not exactly true, he's dimmed a time or two, but when push came to shove, we always knew that we could never survive apart."

She paused in the middle of her chore as her gaze wandered back to the kids. "I know you have to think of Josh, Erica, but you also have to think of yourself. Kids grow up fast. My word, Amber is twelve, and Jeremy is nearly ten. Tina is already four. In less than twenty years, Bob and I are going to look across the breakfast table and realize that it's just us sitting there. The only scenario that I would consider worse is to look across the table and find no one."

"So what are you saying? Throw caution to the wind and pray for the best?"

"No," Laura answered. "What I'm saying is don't be so cautious that you're battened up against a breeze. Alex Harte may not turn out to be your knight in shining armor, but you won't know that if you don't give him a chance."

"That's easy for you to say. You're not the one taking the chance."

Laura dropped the last potato into the pot and patted Erica's shoulder. "Just think how boring life would be if we never took a chance."

ERICA WAS STILL THINKING about Laura's parting words when the phone rang. She grabbed it, convinced it was Alex calling to say he couldn't make dinner, and she couldn't decide if she felt disappointed or hopeful. But when she lifted the receiver to her ear, she didn't even have time to issue a greeting before her mother started in on her.

"Erica, I've been thinking about the My Fair Baby commercials, and even though I understand why you don't want me involved, you're making a big mistake. I have eleven years of experience under my belt. I know how to handle these people and . . ."

"Mother, I don't have time to talk," Erica said when her mother paused long enough to draw a breath. "I have company coming for dinner, so I'll call you tomorrow."

"Who's coming to dinner?" Madelaine asked suspiciously.

"A friend."

"A man friend?"

"Would it make a difference?"

"Of course it would make a difference," Madelaine snapped. "You're in the middle of a custody battle, Erica. You can't afford to give Mark any ammunition against you. You know, sexual mores and all that."

"I hardly think serving meat loaf to a man can be construed as licentious," Erica stated dryly.

"It can be if you're not supervised. I'll be right over."

"Mother!"

"Erica, I'm only thinking of what's best for you. Do you want to lose Josh?"

"Of course I don't want to lose Josh, but I'm not going to live my life in a fishbowl, either."

"Well, you're most likely living in one anyway. I wouldn't put it past Mark to have people watching you. I did notice a suspicious-looking car when I left your house yesterday. He probably even has your place bugged."

Erica rolled her eyes toward the ceiling in exasperation. "Bugging my house would be illegal, Mother, but even if Mark has bugged it, he isn't going to get anything worthwhile for the effort. Now, I've got to go. I'll call you tomorrow."

She hung up before her mother could respond and gave a weary shake of her head. Her mother had always been prone to melodrama to get her way, but suggesting that Erica was being watched and that her house might be bugged was a bit much, even for Madelaine. In fact, Erica decided, if she had to suspect Mark of doing anything devious, it would be that he'd hired her mother to drive her crazy.

She checked on the meat loaf and then began to put the finishing touches on the table. She'd nearly completed the task when it dawned on her that she hadn't heard a peep out of Josh for several minutes.

She dropped the silverware in her hand onto the table and ran into the living room, confirming her worst fear. He wasn't watching the tape of *Sesame Street* that she'd put on to keep him occupied.

"Josh, where are you?" she called out as she hurried down the hallway.

"In here," he answered, and Erica blanched when she realized that "here" was the bathroom.

He wouldn't plug up the only toilet in the house tonight, she told herself. Not when Alex was due at any minute. She let out a screech when she burst into the bathroom just in time to see Josh flush half a roll of toilet paper.

"Joshua Thomas Stewart, how many times have I told you not to come in here without telling me?"

He looked up at her with a beaming smile. "But I went all by myself."

Erica's response was a muffled curse as she threw open the linen closet and grabbed the plunger, hoping to divert disaster. As she plopped the tool into the bowl and began to pump it up and down furiously, she told herself that just because it was the third time this week that Josh had pulled this stunt, she couldn't yell at him. He was merely asserting his independence by trying to care for himself. She just wished he'd spend more time concentrating on learning to tie his shoelaces than taking care of his bodily functions.

She finally stopped pumping and eyed the toilet warily, knowing that the only test to find out if she'd saved the day was to flush it again.

Just as she reached for the handle, however, the doorbell rang, and Josh, who'd been standing in the hallway watching her, yelled, "I'll get it," and took off running.

"Josh, you aren't supposed to answer the door alone!" Erica bellowed as she went after him. Even though her house was located in a quiet, respectable neighborhood, it wasn't crime-free. Normally she kept the safety latch in place, but since she was expecting Alex, she'd left it open tonight.

She caught up with her son just as he reached the door, and she linked an arm around his waist and jerked him off his feet. He let out an angry squeal and began to squirm to get away as he yelled, "Let me go!"

"Joshua, I swear that if you don't start obeying the rules, I'm going to lock you in your room and not let you out until you're twenty-one years old," she said as she swung open the door.

Alex grinned when his gaze landed on them. Josh was red-faced with anger, screaming at the top of his lungs and wriggling with the agility of an eel in his mother's arms. Erica was just as red-faced as she struggled to maintain her hold on him and a plunger at the same time.

"Attila the Hun, I presume," he said as he reached out and took the child from her. "What's the problem, Josh?"

"I don't like her," the boy announced, glowering at his mother as he looped his arms around Alex's neck.

"Well, that's tough, because I love you anyway," she snapped. "Even if you do plug up the toilet every other day. Come in, Alex, and make yourself at home. You said you didn't think he was that bad, so you can keep an eye on him while I handle his latest disaster."

With that, Erica pivoted on her heel and marched away, leaving Alex standing in the doorway with a sullen Josh in his arms.

"She's not nice," Josh informed him.

"Mmm," Alex hummed noncommittally as he entered the house and closed the door behind him. Then he asked the boy, "Just what did you put down the toilet?"

Josh grinned at him as he announced, "I went by myself."

"Isn't that something," Alex said as he dropped the boy to his feet. "What's that on television?"

"*Sesame Street*."

"Why don't you watch it while I go help your mother?"

Josh was already so absorbed in the program that he didn't even answer, and Alex headed after Erica.

He found her in the bathroom, pumping the plunger furiously in the toilet and cursing a blue streak. Biting his inner cheek to keep from laughing, he asked, "Should I put in an emergency call to a plumber?"

Erica glanced up at him with a furious look that only made him grin. "Do you know how much a plumber costs?"

"More than a pizza with everything on it?"

"Almost. I swear, I'm going to hide every roll of toilet paper in the house."

"Is that all he's flushed?"

"Isn't that enough?"

Alex stepped into the room and took the plunger from her hands. "When I was his age, it was my mother's favorite nightie. I'll take care of the toilet paper. You'd better take care of the kitchen. Unless my nose deceives me, there is a definite scorching odor coming from that area."

"Oh, no! My meat loaf!" Erica ducked under his arm and took off for the kitchen.

Alex chuckled again as he flushed the toilet and put the plunger into action. As far as dates went, this one was certainly starting out in an unusual manner. Not that this was actually a date, he informed himself. It was more of a mental aberration.

A short time later he had the toilet functioning normally, and he went in search of Erica. She was standing in front of the stove. Since she was unaware of his presence, Alex leaned against the door frame and allowed himself to indulge in a long, lascivious look.

She was barefoot as usual, and the pair of jeans she wore were loose enough for comfort, but well-fitted enough to provocatively display her long legs and softly-rounded bottom. She had on a baggy T-shirt that sported a vampire in an amorous clench with a voluptuous woman. The caption beneath the picture read A Nibble A Day Keeps The Doctor Away.

Alex decided that the vampire had the right idea. He'd like to do a little nibbling on Erica. Starting with the delectable full curve of her bottom lip, and the soft hollow beneath her jaw. He let his gaze glide over her again, while pinpointing a few other areas he'd like to nibble on.

As if sensing his scrutiny, Erica glanced toward him and Alex felt as if he'd been kicked in the gut. Her face was flushed to a rosy hue from the heat, and soft tendrils of damp hair framed her face. Her eyes widened, as if she were startled at finding him in her kitchen, and she flicked her tongue across her lips in a nervous gesture that left them wet and glistening and begging to be kissed.

Alex had never seen a woman look so sexy, and he decided that if the old saying was true that the way to a man's heart was through his stomach, it had nothing to do with food but with the environment. He wanted to stride across the kitchen, push that huge teddy bear cookie jar out of the way and take her right on top of the kitchen counter.

"Has the meat loaf survived or will we be having a requiem?" he asked.

"It has survived," Erica answered breathlessly as she stared at him. Until that very moment she hadn't had a chance to look at Alex, and she decided that even though the man looked great in a suit, he was devastating in a maroon body-hugging T-shirt and a pair of well-worn jeans that displayed muscles in places that she'd only heretofore seen on beefcake posters.

She felt herself blushing when she lowered her gaze and discovered that the placket housing the zipper in his pants was more worn than the rest of the fabric. She'd always been fascinated by the fact that aside from the back pocket of a man's trousers where he kept his wallet, the zipper was always the first to go.

"What can I do to help?" Alex asked, and Erica forced herself to haul her gaze upward. She refrained from waving the pot holder in front of her face when she took note of the glint of hungry sexuality in his eyes and wondered if this was what hot flashes felt like. As far as what he could do to help . . . Well, it just wasn't repeatable in mixed company.

"You could, uh, fill the water glasses. There's a pitcher of ice water in the refrigerator."

"Great," Alex said gruffly. He'd been far too aware of just where Erica's gaze had been centered, and he decided that anything to do with the refrigerator was just what he needed.

He couldn't keep his eyes off her, however, when she opened the oven door and bent to look inside. The denim pulled across her derriere and gave him a view that belonged in an adult bookstore—or at least the thoughts skipping through his mind belonged in one. He wandered blindly in the direction of the refrigerator and had nearly reached it when his feet suddenly went out from under him.

"What the hell?" he yelled as he made a frantic grab for the counter, but his momentum was too great and outside of the action slowing his decent, he landed flat on his back on the floor.

"Alex, are you all right?" Erica cried in alarm as she rushed to him and knelt at his side.

Alex gave a disoriented blink. "What hit me?"

Erica gave him a sheepish look and lifted a plastic toy truck off the floor. "I'm trying to train Josh to put his toys away, but he sometimes forgets. I should have warned you that you always have to watch where you're stepping around here. Are you all right?"

No, he wasn't all right, but his body aches had nothing to do with his fall. What was it about the woman that had him continually riding on the fine edge of lust? She had short curly brown hair, and he liked long, straight blond tresses. She also had a face that belonged on a cereal box or in a laundry commercial, and he'd always preferred an exotic woman. So she had great legs, a kid and reeked of motherhood and family. They were nice traits, but they just weren't on his list of what he needed to pass through life happily.

"Alex, please answer me," she said as she reached out and brushed his hair off his forehead. "Are you okay?"

"No," he said huskily as he reached up and grasped the back of her neck with his hand. As he brought her face toward him, he murmured, "I need a kiss to make me all better."

Erica's heart began to beat so frantically that it was tripping over itself. *This is wrong!* she inwardly railed as his lips came closer. *I can't trust him!*

But she quickly learned that trust was inconsequential when his mouth closed over hers. Her hormones zinged through her body with the speed of a UFO in undetectable flight, and if she'd thought she was hot before, she'd now leaped from the frying pan into the fire.

"So damn soft," Alex whispered as he pulled away from the kiss and gulped in a breath of air.

Before Erica could respond, he was kissing her again, and she braced an arm on either side of his head so he could do with her as he wished. He maintained his hold on her neck with one hand, while the other skimmed down her curves until it cupped her bottom. When he urged her toward his body, gravity alone insisted that she comply.

But even as her elbows began to bend to accommodate his silent request, Josh began yelling, "Mama, come here! Come here! Hurry!"

"What's wrong with him?" Alex muttered as he reluctantly released his hold on Erica.

She stared down at him, her eyes glazed. "He wants me to see something."

Alex would have groaned, but the action would have required far more energy than he had at the moment. He finally understood the old saying of feeling weaker than a newborn kitten. He'd just never realized that it had sexual overtones.

He sighed in resignation when Josh continued to yell for her. "You'd better go see whatever it is he wants you to see."

"Are you sure you're all right?"

He smiled grimly. "There's nothing wrong with me that a moment alone won't cure. Would your finer sensibilities be offended if I asked for the use of your shower and cold-water tap?"

Her low, throaty chuckle made him cover his eyes with his arm. "Go see to the kid," he ordered.

"I'll be back shortly," she murmured as she levered herself away from him.

"A ready-made family is for the birds," Alex grumbled as he sat up on Erica's shiny linoleum. "And maybe it's time I conducted a little investigation into my family tree. Insanity has to be a family trait. If it wasn't, I'd be out of here so fast she wouldn't even see a blur."

But even as he leaned his back against her oak cabinets, he found himself chuckling as he listened to mother and son begin to sing some nonsensical song, their voices out of sync with the television. How many times had his own mother joined him in song as a child? So many times he couldn't even come up with an estimated count.

A pot on the stove began to spit, and Alex pushed himself to his feet and walked to the appliance.

"Another near disaster," he mumbled as he lifted the lid and took note of the fact that the pot had boiled dry. "It's a wonder the kid has managed to survive."

But it wasn't really a criticism, because he remembered the same happenstance occurring in his own home on several occasions during his childhood, and nearly every time a pot had gone up in smoke, it had been because his mother had dropped what she was doing to listen to him.

He tasted the mixed vegetables in the pot, decided that they needed a little doctoring, and then began a search of Erica's kitchen cabinets until he found her hoard of spices and herbs. Whistling in time to the tune Erica and Josh were singing in the other room, he tossed in a little of this and a little of that and added a dollop of water before placing it back on the burner. Then he searched her cupboard drawers for an apron. The first one he came across was some crazy black design with wings attached to it. With a shrug, he put it on and hauled the meat loaf out of the oven.

By the time Erica returned, Alex nearly had dinner ready, and she stood in the center of her kitchen, gaping at the man, unable to decide which she found more startling—the fact that he'd taken over her kitchen, or that he was wearing her bat apron, complete with wings.

He gave her an exaggerated bow and said, "Dinner is nearly served, madam."

The bow would have been far more effective if the wings hadn't flapped. She grinned. "If I'd known that fixing you dinner was this easy, I'd have made your acquaintance years ago."

Alex leaned one hip against the stove and perched his hand on the other. The pose should have looked effeminate, but it was all male confidence. "A guest's work is never done. Of course. I'll expect the same consideration when I cook you dinner at my humble abode."

Erica's heart fluttered, just as it had at the restaurant when he'd told her they'd have to eat out again. She reminded herself of the disastrous end to that evening, but she couldn't forget how he'd showed up a week later disclaiming her suspicions about that steamy kiss they'd shared.

But once burned, twice shy, and even though Erica wanted to take him at face value, she couldn't quite convince herself to do so. She'd given her trust unconditionally to Mark and look what had happened there. Before she ever gave it again, she would be assured that the man was not only sincere, but committed to monogamy.

While she fetched Josh, Alex put the food on the table. Soon they were eating, and she didn't have to worry about conversation, because Josh dominated it. With a new audience at his disposal, he was busy showing off. He counted all the peas and carrots on his plate—aloud. He recited the alphabet and his repertoire of nursery rhymes.

Erica knew she should put a stop to his chattering, but whenever she glanced at Alex, he didn't seem perturbed. In fact, he looked as if he were actually enjoying Josh's antics.

When Josh finally finished his meal, she gave him a cookie and sent him into the living room. Then she and Alex relaxed over a cup of coffee.

"Josh is an extremely bright child," he told Erica as he laced his coffee with cream.

"Is that a polite way of saying your ears are ready to fall off?" she asked in a voice that was half-teasing and half-serious.

He pushed the pitcher toward her. "No. It was a statement of fact. I met a lot of kids his age when we were auditioning for the commercials, and most of them couldn't string a complete sentence together."

She gave a self-conscious shrug, inwardly pleased by the compliment. "I don't think Josh is particularly brighter than most children his age. I just get to spend a lot of time with him. It's one of the perks of being able to work out of my home."

Alex nodded, leaned back in his chair and regarded her over the rim of his cup. "How long have you been divorced?"

"Two years, but it hasn't been long enough," she stated dryly as she poured cream into her coffee and added a pinch of sugar. She tasted it and added another pinch.

"I take that to mean that your divorce wasn't amicable."

"No, it wasn't amicable. What about you? Have you ever been married?"

"Once. It was the longest nine months of my life."

"I take that to mean that your divorce wasn't amicable, either. Any kids?"

"No, thank heavens. Kristen beat me to a pulp as it was. I shudder to think what she would have done if she'd had a kid to bludgeon me with."

"I know exactly what you mean," she muttered so lowly she could have been talking to herself. Then, at a normal conversational level, she said, "Let's talk about something more pleasant, like war in the Middle East."

"You really do have a macabre sense of humor," Alex stated while inwardly chewing on her muttered comment. Intuition told him it was a significant statement, and though he wanted to continue with the conversation, he decided to let it go for now. There'd be other opportunities to explore the meaning behind her words. Besides, she'd raised her hand to brush at her bangs, giving him an excellent view of one high rounded breast crowned with a perky nipple that made him wonder if she was wearing a bra under her T-shirt. He was also assaulted with a strange proprietary feeling. He didn't like the fact that she'd belonged to another man. He didn't like it at all.

Erica gave him a cheeky grin. "It's better than having no sense of humor. Besides, what do you expect from a woman who paints monsters for a living?"

"You've got me there," he said, making himself return her grin. He scooted back his chair, rose to his feet and began to gather the dishes. "Let's get this mess cleared up, and then we can relax and spend some time getting to know one another."

The thought of relaxing with and getting to know Alex sent a shimmer of anticipation through Erica, and she gave a disgusted shake of her head. The man was referring to conversation, and she was going to have to get her mind out of the gutter. It was impossible to have chaste thoughts, however, when everything about the man made her drool, and she once again found her gaze wandering toward his zipper, which was conveniently located at eye level.

"Erica," Alex said, his voice deep and gravelly as he took note of the direction of her stare.

"What?" she murmured as she glanced up at him absently.

Alex nearly dropped the dishes at the dreamy look in her eyes, and he heaved in a deep breath and let it out slowly. Just because she looked like a woman lost in a sexual fantasy didn't mean that she actually wanted to indulge in one, and even if she did, he wasn't going to accommodate her. He'd let his libido rule his life once, and it had ended up in unmitigated disaster. If he ever made love to Erica, which—considering who and what she was—was doubtful, he'd make sure he was in control of himself and the situation.

"You'd better check on the rug rat while I load the dishwasher," he said.

"Just leave the dishes in the sink, Alex. I'll take care of them later," she replied as she rose to her feet and walked toward the living room, deciding that his suggestion to check on Josh was a good one. A few more minutes alone with the man and she might do something that was definitely on a mother's list of no-no's, like attack him right where he stood.

Just the thought of herself doing something so out of character made her smile, but the smile died an instant death the moment she stepped into the living room. Not only was Josh nowhere in sight, but the front door was standing wide open.

6

ALEX'S BLOOD TURNED to ice water when he heard Erica scream, "Josh!" He threw the dishes into the sink and bolted for the living room, arriving just in time to see Erica race out the front door. By the time he caught up with her, she was standing in the middle of the street, tears streaming down her face and her body shaking so badly that he was amazed she was able to remain on her feet.

"Erica, what is it?" he asked as a car careered around the corner and shot toward them. He dragged her to the sidewalk and pulled her into his arms. "Where's Josh?"

"Let me go!" she cried as she struggled to escape his embrace.

"Erica, calm down," Alex ordered, tightening his hold around her when she continued to struggle. "Hysteria isn't going to get us anywhere. Now calm down and tell me exactly what happened so I can help you."

It was the firm tone of his voice that broke through her terror, and Erica bit down on her lower lip. He was right. Hysteria wasn't going to help. She had to be calm and rational. She had to figure out what to do. Josh had been alone for at least ten minutes. By now he could have wandered a good distance from the house.

"I have to call the police," she stated as she once again struggled against Alex's hold.

"Why?" Alex asked, keeping her imprisoned in the circle of his arms.

"Why?" she repeated, her voice once again rising toward an hysterical pitch. She forced herself to draw in a deep breath to regain control. "The front door was standing wide open, and Josh is gone. He could be anywhere, and it'll get dark in another hour or two." New tears pooled in her eyes and began to tumble down her cheeks. "If it gets dark, he'll be so afraid. He's terrified of the dark. That's why I let him sleep with a night-light."

Alex's heart jerked at her words. He, too, had been terrified of the dark as a child, and all those old fears surfaced with ferocity.

"We'll find him before it gets dark," he assured her, wishing he could feel as convinced as he sounded. "But before we call the police, don't you think we should search the house? He may not have come outside."

"Of course he came outside," Erica argued. "He's fascinated with the front yard because it's off-limits. I make him play in the backyard because it's fenced. I usually keep the safety latch on the front door, but I didn't even think about it tonight because . . ."

"Because what?" Alex pushed, knowing exactly what she was thinking and experiencing a surge of anger at the unvoiced accusation—an accusation that he not only knew was accurate, but flooded him with guilt. When she glanced down at her feet instead of answering, he answered for her. "You didn't think about it tonight because you were too wrapped up in me."

"Yes!" Erica spat as she shoved against his chest, finally managing to free herself from his hold. She perched her hands on her hips and glared at him. "My responsibility is to my son, and tonight I forgot that responsibility because of . . . because of . . ."

"Hormones," Alex provided grimly. He raked a hand through his hair. There was a lot more he wanted to say, but Josh was more important. They could confront this issue after the boy had been found.

He took her arm and began walking her purposefully toward the house. "We'll search the house. If he's not inside, then we'll call the police and start a neighborhood search for him. He may be quick, but he's not even three feet tall. His legs will give out before a mile."

Once they entered the house, he closed the door, locked it and threw the safety latch into place. It was a bit like closing the barn door once the horse had gotten out, but at least he felt as if he was doing something constructive.

He turned to face Erica and said, "Search the living room and the kitchen, and I mean every square inch. He could have crawled under a table or into a cupboard. While you do that, I'll hit the bathroom and the bedrooms. I'm serious, Erica. If it's bigger than a bread box, look in it."

"But searching the kitchen is a waste of time," Erica objected. "We were in there all evening, and he didn't come into the room after dinner."

"He may have done so while we were outside. Search both rooms, and if you're done before me, hit the garage."

"We're wasting time!" she repeated angrily. "For every minute we waste, Josh could be getting farther away!"

Alex grasped her shoulders and gave her a shake. "Erica, the police will search the house if we don't. If we can guarantee that Josh isn't here, then they will immediately hit the streets. We're saving time by not wasting it. Now please, start a search."

Erica wanted to continue to argue with him, but her common sense surfaced. Alex was right. It would only take a few minutes to search the house, and if Josh wasn't here, then they could verify that fact. She pulled away from him and walked to the entryway closet.

When Alex was convinced that she was actively searching for the boy, he headed down the hallway. Outside of the linen closet, there wasn't any place for the child to hide in the bathroom, and he went to the next room.

He'd no more than entered it than he knew it was Erica's bedroom. There was a canopy bed covered with frothy lace, and if that hadn't been a dead giveaway, the sedate cotton nightie thrown across a nearby chair was. Alex checked under her bed and in her closet. Nothing.

His stomach began to ache when he walked toward the only other room. It had to be Josh's bedroom, and if he wasn't there, all hell was going to break loose. At first glance, the room was empty and Alex almost walked away, but he forced himself to carry through with the search. As he'd told Erica, if it was bigger than a bread box, then it had to be checked.

Josh wasn't under his bed, nor was he in his toy box, and Alex's stomachache worsened as he approached the closet. If the kid was afraid of the dark, there was no way he'd be in a closet.

As he put his hand on the door handle, he glanced toward the floor and frowned when a tiny white paw shot from beneath it, followed by a cat's irritated yowl. He jerked open the door and a kitten came zooming out of the closet. Alex almost fainted in relief, for Josh was curled in the corner, a flashlight clutched in his arms. He was fast asleep.

"Damn urchin," he muttered as he bent his knees and lifted the boy off the floor. "You scared your mother half to death and nearly gave me a heart attack."

Josh's only response was a soft, adenoidal snore, and Alex chuckled as he carried him to his bed. The kitten began curling around his ankles, and Alex picked it up. It was so small it easily fit in one hand, and he held it close to his face and eyed it suspiciously.

"Why do I get the feeling that you instigated this entire mess?"

The kitten purred and gave his cheek a playful swipe.

Alex dropped the kitten to the bed with the boy and went in search of Erica. He found her in the garage, and she whirled around to face him when he said, "It's okay, Erica. Josh is in his room fast asleep."

For a moment she gazed at him blankly, but as his words sank in she gave him a shaky smile. "He's in his room?"

"Yes. Come and see for yourself."

"He was in his room all the time?" she questioned as she hurried toward the house with Alex trailing after her.

"He was hiding in his closet with a kitten."

She slowed down and looked up at him in confusion when he caught up with her. "A kitten? We don't have a kitten."

"That's what I figured," Alex said as he opened the back door and she entered ahead of him. "He probably saw the kitten outside, opened the door to get it and then took it into his room to hide it. We won't know exactly what happened until he wakes up, and considering the way he's sawing wood, that probably won't happen until tomorrow morning."

Erica barely heard his words. She was too anxious to see Josh and prove to herself that he was all right. When she entered his room, she had to put her hand over her mouth to muffle a sob of relief. He was sound asleep, and a small black-and-white kitten was curled up against his chest.

Erica walked to his bed and brushed the hair off his forehead, resisting the urge to jerk him into her arms and hug the stuffing out of him. Instead, she eased the kitten away from him and began to remove his clothes. Once she had him in his pajamas, she pulled the covers up to his chin and kissed his forehead. Then she lifted the kitten into her hands and frowned at it.

"Who do you belong to?" she asked. It gave a sleepy blink of its eyes, and she put it back on Josh's bed, deciding that she'd solve the mystery of the kitten's ownership tomorrow. Right now, all she wanted was a stiff drink. Unfortunately all she had in the house with any punch to it was a diet cola with caffeine.

She discovered, however, that Alex had another idea in mind. When she walked into the kitchen he was at the stove, and he looked up at her and said, "Go sit down in the living room. I'm making you some hot chocolate. The warm milk will settle your nerves."

Now that the adrenaline rush was over, Erica was so weary that she could barely move, and she did as he'd suggested. Inexorably, the events of the last several minutes began to replay themselves in her mind after she'd collapsed on the sofa, and she automatically reached for her sketchpad.

She was so absorbed in working her agitation out on paper that she was unaware of Alex's presence until he took the pencil from her hand and confiscated her sketchpad.

"Drink your hot chocolate," he said as he settled into the overstuffed chair across from her and began to study the sketch. The image she'd drawn was so monstrous that even in pencil it made Alex's skin crawl.

He tossed the sketchpad to the coffee table and studied her assessingly while she sipped at her milk. When she set the cup down, he asked, "Who is that monster supposed to be? Me?"

The guilty blush that flooded her cheeks gave him his answer. "It's not you specifically," she reluctantly said. "It's what you represent."

"And what, specifically, do I represent?" he asked tautly.

Erica shot him an impatient glare. "You know what I'm talking about."

"No, Erica, I don't."

She raked both hands through her tangled hair. "Why are you making this difficult for me?"

He leaned forward, braced his elbows on his knees and laced his fingers together. "I'm not making this difficult. I would just like to know why you've portrayed me as a monster."

When she didn't respond, he continued with, "I know you feel guilty about what happened with Josh tonight. Hell, I feel guilty, too. But we're both human, Erica, and we make mistakes. We may have behaved irresponsibly, but . . ."

"*May* have behaved irresponsibly?" she interrupted shrilly as she slapped an open palm against the arm of the sofa. When she realized that she might wake Josh, she lowered her voice, but her anger was only emphasized by the lower timbre. "There is no *may* about it! We were so busy looking each other over that we forgot Josh completely. It was just pure luck that nothing serious happened to him, and I'll never forgive myself for that.

"He is my son," she continued adamantly. "I am responsible for him. All you are is some hotshot advertising executive out to make a quick buck. You don't give a damn about us, and you'll forget us the moment your precious commercials are completed, so just get out, Alex. Get out and stay out. We don't need you."

"You don't need me, but you do need my money, don't you?" he taunted. "Why, Erica? Why do you need money so badly that you're willing to put your son to work?"

"That is none of your business," she stated stiffly as she rose from the sofa and crossed to the front door. She threw open the safety latch, unlocked the door and flung it open. "Good night, Alex. I'll see you next Wednesday."

Alex told himself to leave. She was right. All she and Josh were to him was a means to an end, and when the commercials were over, he'd forget about them and move on to the next stage of his life.

But just as he'd convinced himself to make a fast exit, his eyes drifted to her sketch. He was not a monster, dammit!

He rose to his feet and strode toward the door. When he reached it, he slammed it shut and shot the safety latch back into place. Then he pulled Erica into his arms and kissed her for all he was worth.

Erica instinctively began to fight against Alex when his lips came down over hers, but he merely tightened his hold around her and backed her up against the wall. She tried to twist her head free, but he tangled his fingers in her hair and held her head in place. She tried to kick him next, but he levered his thigh between her thighs, rendering her legs useless. She braced her hands against his shoulders and shoved, but he didn't give an inch. She might as well have been trying to move a brick wall.

Tears of impotent fury began to roll down her cheeks, but her anger wasn't directed at Alex. It was directed solely at herself, because, to her horror, her body was responding to his assault. Heat was building in her middle, and her arms were automatically winding around his neck, her fingers burying themselves in the thick thatch of his hair on their own accord.

"That's it," he encouraged hoarsely as he released his hold long enough on her lips to slide one hand beneath her T-shirt to her small, lace-covered breast.

He rocked his thigh against her womanhood, stimulating the hidden nub that was the button to her passion and stroked the peak of her breast with his thumb in a mimicking tempo. She felt as if her body was ready to burst into flame.

She groaned and clenched his buttocks, pulling him closer as she climbed higher and higher, the pleasure-pain building inside her until she hit her limit and exploded. Alex swallowed every one of her small, passionate cries.

"This is what I specifically represent, isn't it?" he asked softly, almost solicitously when he finally released her lips and peered down at her.

Erica nodded in mute response, refusing to look at him. She not only felt humiliated by the way he'd forced her to respond to him, but she was acutely embarrassed by the pressure of his own arousal pressed against her thigh.

"Sex isn't something monstrous, Erica. It's a healthy bodily function."

She released a bitter laugh. She'd heard a hundred variations of that same line from Mark.

"I bet you say that to all the girls," she muttered as she tried to push him away.

Alex caught her chin and stared searchingly into her eyes. "Is that why you keep fighting the chemistry between us? Because you think I sleep around?"

"Come on, Alex. You're a gorgeous single man. You probably have enough notches on your bedpost to write a book of memoirs."

He laughed, and it wasn't a low, throaty laugh. It was a deepbellied guffaw. Afterward, he rested his forehead against hers and said, "Erica, I will admit that I'm not a saint, but I do have enough sense to be discriminatory. And just so you have your facts straight, I don't have enough notches on my bedpost to write a short story, let alone a book of memoirs."

Erica wanted to believe him, because honesty was a basic part of her nature. Unfortunately, so was fidelity, and Mark had taught her the hard way that fidelity wasn't a part of a man's basic nature. As he'd told her time and again, love and lust didn't walk hand in hand, and if man was meant to be monogamous, he wouldn't have such a wanton libido.

Perhaps she could have forgiven Mark his affairs, but she'd never be able to forgive him for the fact that while she lay writhing in anguish in an effort to give birth to their son, he'd been warming another woman's bed and had stayed there even after he'd heard that his wife had given birth to his heir.

"Alex, please let me go."

It was the dull quality of her voice that prompted Alex to do as she'd requested. He'd brought her to release, but he was still aching. If it was up to him, he'd haul her off to bed and deal with the dynamics later. But as she gazed up at him with tears in her eyes he knew they had to deal with them now.

"I need more than this," she stated softly.

"More than what?" he exclaimed impatiently as he raked his hand through his hair. "We turn each other on, Erica. We'd be great together in bed, and we both know it. What is it you want from me? A declaration of undying love?"

"No, but if I make love, it has to mean something. I not only need that for me, but I have a son to consider, and everything that happens in my life extends to his. I want him to grow up with respect for women. I want to teach him that when he makes love, he should do so because his heart demands it, not the front of his pants. The only way I can accomplish those goals is to set a good example, and hopping into bed with you because I find you attractive is not setting a good example. Do you understand what I'm saying, or am I simply wasting my breath?"

"You're not wasting your breath," he stated angrily as he spun away from her and strode across the room. He turned back to face her, his balled fists perched on his hips, which only drew her eyes downward to his obvious arousal and her knees began to tremble.

She locked them in place as she braced her palms against the wall. It would be easy to fall into his arms—far easier than she wanted to admit. And if she didn't have Josh to consider, she knew she'd be dragging Alex toward her bedroom.

But she did have Josh to consider, and she always would.

"I think it's time for you to leave, Alex."

Alex stared at Erica in frustration. He understood everything she was saying. Hell, he even agreed with her, but he didn't want to acknowledge it. He was aching with desire—a desire so hot that he knew he'd be climbing the walls all night. But the only way he could alleviate the ache inside him was to make some kind of a commitment to her, and he'd already tried that path. He'd never be able to trust another woman enough to hand her his heart, and he instinctively knew that that was exactly what Erica would want in the end.

He walked to the door and unlocked it.

"Goodbye, Erica," he said as he walked out without looking back.

"Goodbye," she whispered in response as she watched him walk away.

When he was gone, she closed the door, locked it and then slid down to a sitting position on the floor.

"I'm not going to cry," she whispered as she pulled her knees up to her chest and blinked against the surfacing tears. "I am not going to cry."

And she didn't cry, because she knew she'd made the right choice. So why did she feel so darned miserable about it?

7

ERICA WAS SIPPING her morning coffee when Josh came running into the kitchen. Since he was usually awake before she was, her presence startled him and he skidded to a stop.

"Good morning, Josh," she said. "Did you sleep well last night?"

"Uh-huh," Josh said as he cast a surreptitious look around the room.

"Looking for something?" Erica asked.

"No." He squatted down and squinted his eyes as he searched the floor.

"Are you sure?" Erica said, pulling her robe over the sleeping kitten in her lap when his gaze traveled beneath the table.

"Sure," he mumbled.

"You wouldn't lie to me, would you, Josh?"

"No," he said, gazing up at her through wide blue eyes that were positively angelic in their sincerity.

"Well, I'm glad to hear that, because little boys are supposed to always tell their mother the truth."

When he glanced away guiltily, Erica said, "You know, Josh, I heard a story about a little boy the other day that I just couldn't believe. His mother had told him to never open the front door when she wasn't with him, but do you know what he did?"

Josh shook his head.

"Well, it seems that he saw a kitty outside and he wanted to play with it. He was afraid that his mama wouldn't let him play with it, so he opened the front door when she wasn't around, caught the kitty and then hid in his closet so his mama wouldn't find out what he'd done. Well, when his mama saw the front door open, she got very scared because she thought her little boy had gone outside and something bad had happened to him. She was so scared that she cried, Josh. She cried real hard."

Josh gulped and said, "Can I have some cereal?"

"As soon as I finish the story," Erica answered. "Anyway, a nice man helped the mama look for her little boy, and they found him hiding in the closet with the kitty. The little boy was asleep, so his mama didn't wake him up to scold him, but she was so happy that he was safe and she didn't have to be scared anymore. Do you know what that little boy did the next morning?"

Josh shook his head again.

"When he woke up, he told his mama what he'd done, even though he knew she'd get mad at him. Do you know what his mama did when he told her the truth?"

"Yelled," Josh offered.

Erica bit her inner cheek to keep from laughing. "No, she didn't yell. She told him she was very proud of him for telling her the truth. Then she asked him to never do something like that again, and he promised her he wouldn't, because he loved her very much and didn't ever want to scare her so badly that he made her cry."

When Josh's lower lip began to tremble, Erica asked, "Do you need to tell me something, Josh?" He nodded and she said, "Then why don't you come over here and we'll talk about it."

Josh burst into tears and ran toward her. The kitten, startled awake by the sudden commotion, let out a frightened yowl, leaped off Erica's lap and made a dash for the living room.

Josh's remorse disappeared the moment he saw the cat, and he took off after it, yelling, "Here, kitty, kitty!"

"Joshua Thomas Stewart, you come back here right this instant!" Erica bellowed as she jumped to her feet and ran after her son. "I am not finished talking with you."

"But I want to play with the kitty!"

As boy and cat led her on a merry chase through the house, Erica decided to hell with psychology. When she got her hands on him, she'd turn him over her knee and paddle him.

But when she finally caught up with him, he was sitting in the middle of her bed, hugging the kitten to his chest. He looked up at her with a solemn expression and said, "I'm sorry, Mama. I love you and I don't never want to make you cry."

"Well, it looks as if psychology may be the answer after all," Erica muttered lowly as she sat down beside him and brushed his sleep-tousled hair into place. "You really scared me last night, Josh. Don't you ever open the front door again unless I'm with you, do you understand?"

He nodded and rubbed his cheek against the kitten's head. "Can we keep the kitty?"

Erica's first impulse was to give him an unequivocal no. She knew that Mark hated cats, and if he won custody of Josh, he wouldn't let the boy take the pet with him. It would be cruel to let him form an attachment to the animal only to be separated from it.

But even as Erica reached her conclusions, she found her temper stirring. If she wanted to fight Mark and win, then she had to believe she would win, not subconsciously prepare herself for defeat. And if by some remote chance Mark did manage to beat her, she'd make sure Josh took his pet with him if she had to get a court order to allow him to do so.

"I don't know if we can keep him, Josh," she said as she reached out and scratched the kitten's chin, smiling when it purred loudly at the attention. "It's a baby, so it probably belongs to someone in the neighborhood. We have to try to find out who owns him and give him back to them if they want him."

"But I don't want to give him back!" Josh stated as he tightened his hold around the animal. "He loves me. See?" he prompted when the kitten licked his arm.

"I know, Josh, but if someone owns him, we must give him back." When tears welled in his eyes, she drew his head to her breast and rested her chin on top of it. "If we have to give the kitten back, we'll go to the shelter and get another one, okay?"

"But I don't want another one," he whispered miserably.

"I know, but that may be our only choice. Besides, I'm sure that if we have to give him back, the people will be so happy that you found him that they'll let you come visit with him."

Josh twisted in her arms so he could look up at her. "Yeah?"

"Yeah," she said as she wiped away the tears brimming on his lashes. "Now let's feed you some breakfast. Then we'll get dressed and go see if we can find out who owns the kitty, okay?"

"Okay," he answered, but Erica could tell his heart wasn't in it.

As he crawled off her bed and ambled toward the kitchen, murmuring to the kitten, Erica shook her head and released a heavy sigh. It was at times like this when she missed having a man around, because she knew that if they had to give the kitten back Josh was going to be distraught. It would be so wonderful to have someone who'd put their arms around her, give her a hug and assure her that she'd done the right thing, even if she had broken her son's heart.

But the way her luck was running with men, it was a wish that would probably never come true, so she might as well just prepare herself for an emotional day and march on.

"This is all your fault, Alexander Harte," she grumbled as she followed after her son. "If you hadn't been here, that darn kitten wouldn't have gotten into the house in the first place, and even if it had, I would have at least gotten a good night's sleep so I'd be in fine form to handle the mess. But no, you had to invite yourself to dinner, prance your sexy body around my kitchen, seduce me and then walk out without even so much as a thank-you for feeding you. You probably knew that when I get upset I suffer from insomnia. Well, I hope you're having the same problem."

"What, Mama?" Josh asked, glancing up at her when she walked into the room, still grumbling to herself.

"Nothing, Josh. I was just having a conversation with the most intelligent person I know."

ALEX WAS IN A CHEW-ON-NAILS mood, and he decided to save his staff from the brunt of his temper by spending the morning with Ron editing the film for Susie's commercials.

When he arrived at the studio, he found Ron in his office, his feet up on his desk, a cup of coffee in one hand and a half-eaten doughnut in the other.

"Well, I'm glad to see you're earning your keep around here," Alex stated dryly as he leaned against the doorjamb.

Ron grinned. "Just having my morning dose of sugar so my brain will function properly."

"I thought Claire had you into health food."

"Claire thinks she does, too. I'd offer you a seat, but the only space available is my lap, and it's reserved for pretty girls with long legs and big pectorals."

Alex chuckled. "You'd better not let Claire hear you say that."

"Actually, it might do Claire some good to hear me say that," Ron said with a pensive frown. He downed the remainder of his doughnut. "I keep popping the question, and she keeps saying no."

"You and Claire have been living together in cohabitational bliss for three years. Why screw up a good thing with a marriage license?"

"Tsk, tsk," Ron said, wagging his index finger from side to side in a scolding gesture. "It isn't nice to show your cynicism around a romantic. Besides, if I'm good enough to live with, then I should be good enough to marry."

"Yes, but if the bottom falls out, you don't have to drag your dirty laundry through a divorce court," Alex countered.

"True," Ron agreed. "But the other side of that coin is that if divorce court is the only alternative, you at least make an effort to see if the bottom can be put back into place."

"That isn't always true, and Claire has already been through one divorce. The way I hear it, the first one is always the hardest. After that, it's no more irritation than a hangnail."

Ron rocked his chair back against the wall, braced his feet on the edge of his desk and eyed Alex thoughtfully. "Who are you trying to convince? Me or yourself?"

"You, of course," Alex said with a scowl. "You know I'm not involved with anyone."

"And what about Erica Stewart with the big brown eyes and her adorable munchkin that would make any normal man develop a thirst for fatherhood?"

"Good heavens, you're not only a romantic, but you're suffering from delusions," Alex muttered. "All you'd have to do is spend one evening in the Stewart home and any thirst for fatherhood would definitely be quenched."

Ron let out a hoot of laughter. "I knew it! If you've spent an evening at her house, you're smitten."

"Smitten?" Alex repeated in disgust. "What kind of a word is that for a grown man to use? If anything I'm . . . I'm . . . Hell, I don't know what I am, but it certainly isn't smitten."

"Don't get so tensed up about it," Ron said as he dropped his feet to the floor and walked over to Alex. He put his arm around Alex's shoulders in a gesture of camaraderie. "Take it from a man who's already been there. You just shut down the thought processes and let everything happen at its own natural pace. However, when you hit the point that you know you're going to die if you don't wake up every morning with *that* woman by your side, it's time to put the old brain matter back to work. Don't get yourself into the same mess I'm in. Put a ring on her finger and make her order a wedding cake."

"You're nuts," Alex muttered as he shrugged off his friend's arm. "I'm *not* smitten, and it will be one sweltering day at the North Pole before I ever get married again. Now, let's get to work. Susie's commercials aren't going to put themselves together by themselves."

"Slave driver," Ron said good-naturedly as he led the way to the editing room.

But when they were working on the film, Alex found his mind wandering away from the project at hand and to the Stewarts. How had Erica handled Josh this morning when she confronted him about his little escapade last night? What had she done with the kitten? Would she let the boy keep it?

He hoped so, because he remembered how he'd longed for a pet as a kid. Unfortunately their apartment building hadn't allowed pets, and even though his mother had always vowed that someday they'd live in a house with a yard and a fence where he could have as many pets as he wanted, it had been just one more fantasy that she'd spun for herself to make her life of drudgery more palatable.

As always, the thought of the good life his mother had given up for him caused a deep stab of guilt. He knew in his heart that she had never resented him for it, but he'd never be able to forget how hard it had been for her to go it alone. Just as Erica was trying to go it alone with Josh.

The thought made him stiffen to his chair, and he forced himself to concentrate on the film Ron was editing while telling himself that Erica's circumstances weren't the same as his mother's. It was evident that she wasn't drowning in money, but it was also evident that she wasn't struggling to survive, either. She had a mother and an ex-husband to help carry the load, so she wasn't going it alone.

But even as he bolstered up his hypotheses, doubt began to creep in. If she wasn't struggling for money, then why had she put Josh to work? If she and her mother had a good relationship, then why had her mother gone behind her back to audition Josh? And finally, why did she perceive her attraction to him as something monstrous? Did it have something to do with her ex-husband, and if so, what had he done to cause it?

There were too many questions and not enough answers, and Alex told himself to let well enough alone. Last night, Erica had made it clear where her priorities lay. She wasn't the run-of-the-mill model or career woman he ran across who was interested in a temporary liaison. She was a mother with a mother's responsibilities, and as she should be, she was looking for a man willing to take on the role of husband and father.

Since Alex wasn't in the market for either role, he'd treat Erica like he did every other business associate. He'd be polite and friendly and talk about the weather.

Fat chance. If he really believed he could treat Erica like any other business associate, then he might as well invest in a time-share condominium on the moon.

ERICA KNEW THAT LIFE wasn't a bowl of cherries, but she'd spent the last few days wallowing in the pits. The only good thing that had happened—and she was using the term loosely—was that Josh's kitten had turned out to be from a litter of five, and the family had been eager to turn him—her—over to a good home.

Now, Kitty, as Josh had so eloquently named her, had become a member of the household. So had her litter box, which took up the space where the clothes hamper was supposed to sit. Erica decided that she was nearly ready to sell her soul for a two-bathroom house as she herded Josh and Kitty toward the front door. They were due at the studio in twenty minutes, and she had a thirty-minute drive ahead of her.

She'd just put her hand on the door knob when the phone rang. She told herself to ignore it, but a ringing phone always drove her nuts. She really *was* going to have to invest in an answering machine, she told herself.

"Erica, you're still at home?" her mother gasped in disbelief when she answered. "You're supposed to be at the studio in . . ."

"I know when I'm supposed to be at the studio, Mother, but I'm running late. What do you want?" Madelaine coughed delicately, which made Erica narrow her eyes suspiciously. "You were checking up on me. Why?"

"I, uh, just wanted to make sure you were on your way to the studio. It's not professional to be late, Erica."

"Mother, Josh and I are not professionals. He's contracted to do one commercial, and if I feel he's up to it, he will do the other three. However, as soon as the film is in the can, he is going into retirement—permanently."

"But, Erica . . ."

"This issue is not open for discussion, and I swear, Mother, if you show up at the studio, Josh and I will walk off the set."

"But that's not fair! I got Josh this job, and I should be a part of it."

Erica closed her eyes and counted to ten. "You got Josh this job behind my back, and after I had already told you that you couldn't audition him."

"And if I hadn't gone behind your back, where would you be? Up a creek without a paddle. You need the money and you know it. You said yourself that your lawyer said . . ."

"I know what my lawyer said, Mother. I also know that I'm running late. Now, I can stand here and belabor all the points we've argued about for the past few days, or I can head for the studio. It's your call."

"Erica, I don't know what's gotten into you. You used to be so . . ."

"Milk toast is the description you're looking for," Erica stated laconically. "And what has gotten into me is a few assertiveness training courses. You're my mother, and I love you, but Josh is not a commodity. He's your grandson, so instead of trying to chase your fame-crazed dreams, why don't you just sit back and enjoy him?"

"Do you really hate me that much?" Madelaine asked in a tear-choked voice.

Erica shook her head in defeat, unable to discern if the tears were true or fake. Her mother could turn on her tears as quickly as a faucet could shed water, but she also knew that despite the hard, outer shell that Madelaine displayed to the world, she was extremely vulnerable. It was that vulnerability that had kept her father hanging on to their marriage when any other man would have walked away.

"I'll offer you a deal," Erica finally said. "If you really want to help—and if you're willing to accept that once the My Fair Baby commercials are over Josh goes into retirement—you can attend the studio sessions. But if you have grandiose dreams of a career for him, then stay at home.

"We could use your moral support, Mother, but I am in control. I am Josh's mother, and as such, I will decide what he will or will not do. Again, it's your call. Think over what I've said, and if you're amenable to my conditions, meet us at the studio."

Erica hung up without waiting for a response and cursed when she discovered that Josh and his kitten had wandered away. Wasn't it enough that she had to put up with Mark and his insane custody battle? Why was her mother laying on the guilt so thick that Erica could have made a ham sandwich out of it?

"Josh, where are you?" she asked impatiently.

"In here," he announced. "Kitty had to go."

Erica buried her face in her hands and wondered if she should join the Hemlock Society.

ALEX HAD WORKED himself up for his next meeting with Erica. In fact, he'd even rehearsed their entire time together. They'd exchanged a few pleasantries, he'd turn her and Josh over to wardrobe and makeup. Then, when the boy was ready, he'd settle Erica on the sidelines with a cup of coffee. Afterward, they'd exchange a few more pleasantries, and he would go his way while she went hers.

But he soon discovered that the best-laid plans of mice and advertising executives were destined to go astray. First, his secretary called to say that Erica had called to say that she was running late. Alex wasn't particularly pleased by the message. The camera crew was hired to start at 10:00 a.m. sharp, and they got paid whether Josh was ready or not. But Erica was on her way, so he wasn't going to lose his cool.

The next thing he knew, however, Erica's mother swept into the studio, and Alex hadn't spent five minutes with the woman before he was certain the entire project was doomed. Madelaine Harris had something to say about everything from the location of the cameras, to the pile of toys, to even—heaven forbid—actual criticism over the quality of My Fair Baby clothing, which he happened to know was of impeccable quality.

By the time Erica arrived, he was ready to kiss her for coming to his rescue. After all, Madelaine was her mother. She could tell the woman what to do with her suggestions and criticisms and get away with it.

But Erica not only looked harried today, she looked as if she were about to collapse. In the few days since he'd last seen her, she'd developed circles beneath her eyes, her lips were pinched and he'd swear she'd lost weight.

"Erica, are you all right?" he asked as he cautiously approached her.

She glanced up at him and gave a disgusted shake of her head. "Of course, I'm not all right. I'm a mother, remember? How do you feel about animals in your commercial?"

"Animals?" he repeated inanely.

She pushed Josh forward. "Where Josh goes, Kitty goes, and vice versa. If I had to make a diagnosis, I'd say it's a definite psychosis. By the way, do you have a litter box on the set?"

"A litter box?"

"Sandbox, Alex. It's short and square and handles a kitten's accidents."

Alex didn't know if it was nerves or outright humor that hit him. All he knew was that he started to chuckle, the chuckle deepened to a laugh, and then he was roaring with hilarity. One look at Erica's frowning countenance told him that she hadn't gotten the punch line, but he couldn't stop laughing long enough to explain it to her. He'd spent hours—days—preparing himself for a professional encounter, only to have the woman walk in and demand a litter box!

"Care to share the joke?" she asked irritably when he'd finally managed to regain control.

He shook his head. "I think you had to be there." He turned his attention on her son. "That's a gorgeous cat, Josh. What's his name?"

"Kitty, and she's a . . . a . . ."

"Girl," Erica muttered. "It's going to cost me twice as much to get her fixed as it would a boy, which would be an easy snip here and an easy snip there and it would be over."

Alex winced. "That sounds so bloodthirsty."

"According to the vet, it's humane," Erica mumbled as she peered around him. "Oh, darn. Mother's here. Is she behaving herself?"

"I think that would depend on how you define misbehavior."

Erica shook her head in resignation. "I told her she had to behave, but I should have known she wouldn't listen to me. Between her and these two, I think I should pack my bags and run away from home. How do you feel about adoption, Alex? I have a three-year-old son with very few miles on him, and a kitten with even fewer miles. It'd be a great buy. In fact, it would be a steal. I'd even *pay* you to take them."

Alex stuffed his hands into his pockets and rocked back on his heels. "Well, I might consider it if you'd be willing to throw in a year's supply of toilet paper."

"A year's supply?" Erica yelped. "What are you trying to do? Bankrupt me?"

Alex smiled. "Hey, I might not be the brightest man to come along, but I didn't fall off a turnip truck, either."

"Boy, do you drive a hard bargain. I guess I'm just going to have to keep them." She reached down and smoothed Josh's hair into place. "I was serious, Alex. What Josh and Kitty have going is some heavy kind of bonding. I don't think I can pry them apart. Maybe we should set up a new shooting date."

Alex's smile became an instant frown. "Are you trying to back out of your contract, Erica?"

"No," she denied so quickly that he knew it was the truth. "I'm merely giving you the facts."

Alex peered down at the boy, disconcerted. The commercials he had planned certainly didn't include animals—at least none that weren't made out of fake fur.

"I think we need to consult with Ron." He glanced around the studio in search of the director. "He was here just a minute ago. I wonder where he went?"

"If I had to lay odds, as far away from my mother as possible," Erica stated with a long-suffering sigh. "You find Ron, and I'll see if I can hog-tie Madam Goldwyn. Come along, Josh."

"No," Josh said stubbornly as he backed away from her. "I want Alex."

Erica didn't know whether to scream or to cry when she faced her son. Over the past few days he'd become more contrary than normal, and even though it was maddening, she also suspected he was picking up on her distress. The closer her appointment with the lawyer had come, the more nervous she'd become. After her meeting with him yesterday, she'd discovered that her nervousness had been completely justified.

"It's all right, Erica," Alex said as he lifted boy and cat into his arms. "I'll keep an eye on him."

"I'm sorry about all this, Alex," she said.

"It's okay," Alex murmured as he reached out and brushed a curl away from her cheek. She looked so disconsolate that he wanted to give her a hug. "You look beat. Why don't you sit down and have a cup of coffee? Ron and I will deal with Kitty and Madam Goldwyn."

Erica's sense of responsibility told her she couldn't take him up on his offer. As her mother would say, it wasn't professional. She'd signed a contract guaranteeing Alex a commercial, and he'd paid her on the spot. She was the one who should be playing baby-kitty-sitter and lion tamer, not him.

But Alex was right. She was beat. In fact, she was exhausted both physically and mentally. She'd been telling herself that her recurring insomnia had to do with the stress of the custody battle, but as she stared up at Alex, she admitted that a good deal of it had to do with him.

It was wrong, but she wanted him, and she suddenly realized that it wasn't just sex. Alex was a strange mixture of strength and vulnerability. When she was with him, his strength made her feel safe. His vulnerability made her want to nurture him, and that nurturing didn't have one ounce of motherly overtones.

"That's the best offer I've had all day," she said in answer to his suggestion.

Then she turned and walked away from him, worrying at her bottom lip with her teeth, because Erica had also suddenly realized that it would be very easy to fall in love with Alexander Harte.

8

EXCEPT FOR THE POOL of light over the set, the studio was dark, and a lump formed in Erica's throat as she watched Josh swagger across it. He was wearing dark green trousers made out of fabric developed by My Fair Baby, who claimed it was as sturdy as denim, but as lightweight as cotton, and a bright yellow T-shirt with a teddy bear being lifted into the air by balloons on the front.

As Ron had instructed him, Josh was dragging a bright red ball of yarn. His eyes were lit with mischief and he kept casting furtive looks at Kitty, who was entertaining herself with a tiny ball of crumpled-up paper.

The kitten finally spotted the yarn and she went into a crouch, her rump up in the air and her tail switching from side to side as though she were a racing car revving herself up at the starting line. Josh began to watch her expectantly and when she pounced, he was ready for her. They ended up in a tug-of-war over the yarn and, as Ron had planned it, the loose knot came undone, allowing the cat to take off with the ball. Josh chased her, trying to get the ball back, and soon boy and cat were tangled up in yards and yards of yarn. Josh collapsed on the floor, roaring with laughter, at which time the kitten jumped on his chest and began to rub its head against his face.

"I knew it," Madelaine murmured beside her. "He's a natural. He did everything the way Ron told him to do it, and he did it perfectly. He should be enrolled in acting lessons. Modeling could be just the beginning for him."

Erica wanted to adamantly dispute her mother's words, but she found she couldn't, because she actually believed that the woman might be right for once. Josh was not only on center stage and commanding it, but he appeared to be loving every moment of it.

She started in surprise when Alex, who was standing behind her, laid his hand on her shoulder. She glanced up at him, and though his face was shadowed, there was enough light for her to see the concerned expression on his face.

"Would you like some more coffee?" he asked, but Erica knew he was really asking her if she was all right.

"I'm fine," she murmured.

"You're sure?"

"I'm sure."

But when he began to withdraw his hand, Erica found herself placing her hand over his to keep it in place. She'd spent the past few weeks convincing herself that Josh would hate this world as much as she had hated it, and now all her convictions were being blown apart. She needed his touch to help her deal with that fact. As if instinctively understanding what she was seeking, he placed both hands on her shoulders and gave them a reassuring squeeze.

Alex had known that Josh was going to be wonderful, but even he was amazed at just how good the kid was. He was going to have to clear the use of Kitty in the commercial with his client, but it appeared that Josh's attachment to his new kitten was going to be a windfall. Their play activities gave the exact rough and tumble image that he'd wanted to project for My Fair Baby's new line of play clothes.

The next two hours flew by as Ron coached boy and kitten through variations of the same game, and Alex blinked in surprise when the lights came on. He wasn't surprised, however, by the reaction of the crew. Every adult in the room crowded around the boy and his kitten, with the exception of Erica, who was sitting so still in her chair that she could have been carved from stone.

Alex moved in front of her and extended his hand to help her to her feet. "Shall we go rescue Josh from his horde of fans?"

If Erica saw his hand, she ignored it. She was staring at the crowd surrounding the set. "He was good, wasn't he?"

"Yes, Erica," Alex replied. "In fact, Josh was more than good. He was excellent."

She gave him a puzzled look. "I was so sure he'd hate all of this, but he appears to be so...so self-confident up there."

"Why does that surprise you?" Alex asked as he crouched down in front of her in order to see her face clearly.

She didn't answer him. Instead, she asked, "Do you want us back here at the same time tomorrow?"

Alex frowned, sensing that she was deeply distressed, but he couldn't force her into talking to him, could he? Still he wanted to try.

"No. Ron and I have to work up a presentation for the people at My Fair Baby. We'll have to get their permission to use Kitty in the commercial, and if we can meet with them tomorrow, we can resume shooting on Friday."

"I'm sorry we've created such a hassle," Erica stated with a miserable sigh.

"Well, I'm not sorry," Alex stated staunchly. "If Josh and Kitty look as good on film as they did on the set, we're going to have an even better commercial than I'd planned. However, if My Fair Baby agrees to this change, you and I will have to renegotiate our contract."

"Renegotiate it? Why?" Erica questioned suspiciously. If Alex thought he was going to reduce the amount of money they'd agreed upon because Josh was refusing to work without his kitten, then the man had a definite surprise in store for him.

"We need to include Kitty," he said. "I don't know how much animal acts are getting paid these days, because I haven't used any of them for more than a year, but..."

"You want to *pay* me for Kitty?" Erica interrupted in disbelief.

"It is standard practice, Erica."

"Talk about receiving pennies from heaven," Erica murmured softly as she transferred her gaze to the set. Most of the crew had left, and Josh was sitting in his grandmother's lap while she was engaged in deep conversation with Ron. He was slumped in his chair, petting Kitty, who was sprawled across his chest, and even though his expression clearly indicated that he wasn't particularly pleased about whatever Madelaine was saying, he didn't look as if he were ready to duck into the shadows, either. "I'd better go rescue Ron from Mother before she wears out her welcome," she said, rising to her feet.

Alex also stood, and he caught her arm before she could walk away. When she looked up at him in question, he asked, "What's wrong, Erica?"

"Nothing's wrong," she said, quelling the impulse to jerk away from his touch. During the filming it had been reassuring to have his hands on her, but now it was disturbing.

Alex clenched his teeth at her lie. Even if he hadn't already suspected that something was wrong, he would have after her murmured comment about pennies from heaven. He was tempted to drag her to Ron's office, pull her into his arms and thoroughly seduce her to get his answers. The trouble was, he had a feeling that by the time he had her compliant enough to give them to him, he would have forgotten the questions.

He released her arm and stuck his hand into his pants pocket, jingling his change. He was still trying to decide whether or not he wanted to pursue the subject when Josh ran up to his mother.

"Can me and Kitty spend the night with Grandma?" he asked her.

"Oh, I don't know, Josh," she said. "You don't have your pajamas, and Kitty doesn't have her litter box."

"I have an extra set of pajamas at my house," her mother announced as she joined them. "And we can stop at the store for a box for Kitty."

Erica eyed her mother in distrust. It certainly wouldn't be the first time Josh had spent the night with her, but it would be the first time he'd done so after filming a commercial. She recalled all too well her mother's highs after a successful shoot, and there was no telling what she'd do. By morning she could have taken him to a half dozen more auditions.

But even though she wanted to say no, she found she couldn't as she gazed down into Josh's expectant face. Her mother wouldn't dare go behind her back again, she assured herself, and if her earlier assertion that Josh was more unruly than normal because of her mood, it would probably do him good to spend a night away from her.

"All right," Erica agreed reluctantly. "But I need him home early tomorrow, Mother."

"We'll be there bright and early," Madelaine said as she bid Alex goodbye, took Josh's hand and led him toward the wardrobe room to change.

"It looks as if you're going to have some time where you can sit back and relax," Alex commented.

Erica gave him a grim smile. "What I'm going to have is some time where I can concentrate on my work. I have two deadlines looming and neither project is near completion."

"You should at least get to bed early tonight," Alex said as he resisted the urge to reach out and touch the bruises beneath her eyes. "You look exhausted."

"I've had a rough few days. You know, introducing a new member into the household, etcetera."

"How about lunch?" Alex found himself asking. "We could pick up a quick bite somewhere close by."

"Thanks, but no," Erica demurred. "I really have too much to do."

"It would be strictly business," he said, accurately assessing the reason for her refusal.

She met his gaze, and the banked sexuality glinting in his eyes made her long to step into his arms. Her life was in such a turmoil, and it would be so wonderful to forget all her worries and lose herself in the passion simmering between them. The problem was, not only would all her worries be waiting for her when it was over, but she had a feeling that she would have lost her heart to Alex. Since she already knew he was interested in nothing more than an affair, she couldn't take the risk.

"It wouldn't be strictly business, and we both know it," she told him. "Let's just keep things the way they are. It's less complicated that way."

Alex started to disagree with her, but Ron came bounding up to them.

"Man, do we have some work ahead of us," he told Alex as he rubbed his hands together in eager anticipation. "But if we can sell the people at My Fair Baby on what we've done today, our tickets are written."

Before Alex could respond, Ron said to Erica, "Josh is going to be the hottest thing to hit the market in years, Erica. If you play your cards right, you'll be able to set him up for life. Hell, he's so damned talented that you may have a male Shirley Temple on your hands."

Erica could feel the color draining from her face, and she forced a weak smile. "I'm glad you're so pleased with Josh, Ron. I think I'd better be going. I'll see you both Friday unless I hear otherwise."

Alex cursed lowly as she all but ran out of the studio.

ALEX TOLD HIMSELF that his reasons for showing up at Erica's house were strictly business. He and Ron had spliced together a portion of film that would knock the socks off a child-hater. He'd be giving the presentation to My Fair Baby tomorrow afternoon, and he had no doubt that My Fair Baby would approve. But for some inexplicable reason he wanted Erica's opinion on the film before he showed it to his client.

He'd tried to call her from the studio for several hours, only to get a busy signal. Since Josh was at her mother's and she'd said she had a lot of work to do, he assumed that she'd taken the telephone off the hook.

But when night began to fall and her phone was still busy, Alex knew something was terribly wrong. Erica was a devoted mother. Josh wasn't at her side, so she'd make herself available to come to him in an emergency.

The house was dark when he arrived, and so was her garage, which meant she wasn't working in her studio. Maybe she'd done as he'd suggested. Maybe she'd gone to bed early.

Alex didn't believe one word of it. He walked to her door and leaned on the doorbell.

"What do you want?" Erica demanded when she finally flung open the door.

Her eyes were red and swollen, and Alex grabbed the edge of the door when she tried to slam it in his face. He forced himself inside.

"What's wrong?" he demanded as he slammed the door behind him. "And don't give me any more soft soap, Erica. There are many things I'll tolerate from a woman, but lying isn't one of them."

"Why should it matter if I lie to you? There isn't anything between us," she shot back.

Alex leaned his weight against the door, momentarily poleaxed. She was right. There wasn't anything between them, so why should it matter if she lied to him?

The hell there wasn't anything between them! he immediately corrected as his temper flared. He'd been in perpetual heat almost from the moment he'd laid eyes on her, and he knew that she was suffering from the same malady. They could fight against it until doomsday, but the only certain cure for both of them was going to be a good tussle beneath the sheets.

He took a step toward her, and she took a step back.

"I want you to leave, Alex."

"No," he said. "I'm not leaving, because you want me to stay, Erica. You want me to kiss you. You want me to touch you. You want me to make love to you."

She pressed her hands over her ears and screamed, "I do not!"

Two long strides brought him to her, and he pulled her hands away from her ears. "You do, too. You want me as much as I want you. Why are you fighting it?"

She burst into tears, and Alex pulled her head to his chest. He held her close as she soaked his shirt. The tears he could have handled, but it was Erica's heart-wrenching sobs that got to him. She wasn't crying. She was grieving. Why?

He carried her to the big oak rocking chair that sat in front of the windows and settled her on his lap. Then he rocked her and stroked her hair with the same tender solicitousness that he'd give a wailing child. The only light in the room was a neighbor's porch light, which filtered weakly in through the windows, and Alex stared into the darkness while his mind churned, trying to analyze the jumble of emotions he was experiencing. When he'd walked into her house, he'd done so with lust in his heart, but now he was being overwhelmed with feelings of concern and worry—with a compelling need to comfort and, heaven help him, protect.

It was the last realization that sent panic rushing through Alex, because he knew that when a woman began to draw on a man's protective instinct, it was only a matter of time before he went down for the count. If he had one ounce of common sense—hell, if he had one ounce of self-protective instinct—he'd get out of here now. Right this instant. Posthaste.

He sighed and relaxed more deeply into the chair.

Eventually Erica stopped crying, and she was so still in his arms that he suspected she'd gone to sleep. When he shifted into a more comfortable position, however, she said, "Do you want me to get up?"

"No." He rested his cheek against her hair in resignation. He was definitely getting ready to go down for the count. "What I want is for you to tell me what's wrong. Something's troubling you, Erica, and I can't help you if I don't know what it is."

"There's only one way you can help me," Erica said, rolling her head to his arm so she could look up at him. "Make love to me, Alex. Make love to me so I can forget for a while. I want to forget everything and feel. Please, just make me feel."

Five minutes ago, Alex would have instantly complied with her request, but five minutes ago, Erica hadn't been sobbing her heart out against his chest.

He tenderly brushed the clinging hair away from her damp cheeks. "I'm sorry, Erica, but I can't."

"You don't want me?" she asked tremulously.

"Oh, I want you," he confessed, giving her a fierce hug to add emphasis to his words. "I want you more than I've ever wanted a woman, but I don't want to be used. When we make love—and we will make love—I want it to be for all the right reasons. Not because I'm some sort of placebo that will make you forget. I want—need—more than that, Erica. I have to be sure that you're fully aware of me."

She placed her hand against his heart. "I am aware of you. Totally aware of you. Your heart is beating as rapidly as mine. Your breath is just as shallow and fast." She slid her hand lower, cupping him. "You're aching for me as much as I'm aching for you."

Alex cursed and grabbed her wrist, jerking her hand away from his arousal. He loosened his grip when she grimaced, while stating tightly, "My ex-wife used me, Erica, and I will not allow myself to be used again. If you want me, then you are going to confide in me. A relationship is not a one-way street. It's built on sharing. It's built on trust."

"We don't have a relationship."

"Well, we're going to have one, and it's starting right now. You wanted a commitment, lady, and I'm giving you one. Now tell me what the hell is going on."

Erica bounded out of his lap at the order and began to pace the room. Alex was tempted to go after her—to drag her back into his arms where he could control her—but he forced himself to remain seated. Thankfully he was able to release his tension by rocking, and he set the rocking chair into motion.

She was silent for so long that he didn't think she was going to confide in him, but at the very moment he decided it was time he just gave up and left, she said, "Mark is trying to take Josh away from me."

"Mark is Josh's father?"

Erica nodded.

"Why is he trying to take Josh away from you?" he asked.

Erica stopped pacing and gave a miserable shake of her head. "He wants to get back at me for leaving him. Mark has a huge ego. He's never accepted the fact that I walked out instead of waiting for him to throw me out. And he would have eventually thrown me out. I was just a passing fancy in his life. In fact, I think he probably only married me because he knew that was the only way he was going to get me into his bed, and what Mark wants, Mark gets. Now he wants Josh."

Alex slowed his rocking as he absorbed her words. Finally, he said, "I know California is liberal, but I think they're still pretty traditional when it comes to child custody, at least with a child as young as Josh. Unless Mark can actually prove that you're an unfit mother, he probably doesn't have a snowball's chance in hell of winning."

"That's just it," Erica whispered as she swiped at a new bout of tears. "He thinks he can prove me unfit."

Alex was instantly on his feet and pulling her into his arms. "Don't be ridiculous, Erica. I haven't been around you and Josh that much, but I have been around enough to know that you're a wonderful mother. No judge is going to turn him over to your ex-husband."

"I wish you'd tell that to my attorney," she stated miserably as she rested her forehead against his chest. "He met with Mark's attorney this afternoon to see if we could settle out of court, and the man wouldn't even discuss the issue. He's going to win, Alex. I know he's going to win. I feel so helpless."

"There are a lot of words I'd use to describe you, Erica," Alex muttered as he smiled down at her encouragingly, "but helpless isn't one of them." He arched her back, pulling her against him.

Erica's mind and body responded instantly. But it wasn't sex she craved. It was love. But love and sex were not synonymous. Alex had said he was giving her a commitment, but how long would it last? A day? A week? A month?

Until the commercials are over, her conscience provided. Was that enough? No, it wasn't enough, and even though she wanted to wind her arms around his neck and give in to him she knew she couldn't.

"It's time for you to leave, Alex," she said as she backed away from him.

"That line is getting old, Erica. In fact, it's gone beyond old. You don't want me to leave, and you know it."

"All right, I'll admit it," she stated angrily as she glared at him. "I don't want you to leave. I want you to throw me over your shoulder and carry me off to bed. We'll have a good roll in the hay, Alex, but what will we have when it's over?"

"A good memory, and hopefully, a desire for more of the same," he stated just as angrily. "I'd like to tell you that we're going to stretch in each other's arms and vow an undying love, but life isn't that uncomplicated. There are no guarantees, Erica. We've both learned that, and we've learned it the hard way. All I can offer you is a chance. Take it or leave it."

She spun away from him and raked her hands through her hair. Chances were for fools, and she knew it.

"Why did you and your wife get a divorce?" she asked.

"Two reasons," he answered tightly. "One evening she pranced into the living room, and while she was painting her toenails, she announced that she'd been to the doctor because she thought she was pregnant. Luckily she wasn't, because she said that if she had been she'd have had an abortion. I think her exact words were that she just wasn't into motherhood and into pain even less. She said she'd rather die than give birth."

Erica spun back around to face him, her horror reflected on her face. "And the second reason?" she asked weakly.

"Kristen worked for a rival advertising firm. We were competing on the same account. She stole my ideas, which got her a vice presidency and cost me my job." His smile was more of a grimace. "I loved Kristen, Erica. I didn't marry her for the kids we'd have, and I was willing to try to accept her aversion to motherhood. I couldn't, however, accept the fact that she would steal from me."

"Oh, Alex," Erica murmured consolingly. She came to him and rested her hand against his chest. The way it rose and fell beneath her touch told her volumes. Like her, he'd been hurt. So very, very hurt. Suddenly she needed to take that hurt away in the most basic of ways.

"Make love to me," she whispered urgently as she stood on tiptoe and pressed her lips to his.

"I don't want to make love to you," he stated tautly as he pulled away from the kiss. "I want to make love *with* you." He caught her face in his hands and stared down at her compellingly. "It's your choice, Erica. We do it together, fully aware of what is happening, or I walk out the door. As I said, I won't be used as a placebo to help you forget."

He'd thrown down the gauntlet and Erica knew that she either had to pick it up or walk away. She was torn, because, as he'd said, there were no guarantees. They could wake up tomorrow and decide that it had all been a mistake. Or they could wake up tomorrow and decide that there might be a future.

All her doubts—her insecurities—tumbled through her mind. She had to think of Josh, but as Laura had so succinctly reminded her, in less than twenty years, Josh would be gone. Did she want to wake up one morning, look across the breakfast table and find that no one was there?

She wrapped her arms around Alex's neck and kissed him again before murmuring, "I hope you won't be turned off by my stretch marks."

"Stretch marks?" he mumbled unintelligibly as he kissed her back.

She nodded. "When I was pregnant with Josh, I got to be as big as a house."

Alex pressed a hand against her flat abdomen. "If you're going to talk that sexy, then you'd better be ready to handle the consequences."

"Speaking of consequences," Erica murmured between ardent kisses. "Are you prepared for this?"

"I've carried protection in my wallet since I was fifteen," he stated roughly as he wrapped his arms around her and pulled her close.

And then he did for her what she'd asked for earlier. He made her feel. And Erica had to admit that she was fully aware of him as he undressed her. Where his hands touched, she burned. When his lips followed, she burst into flame.

But it wasn't just his lovemaking that inflamed her. It was his tenderness. His gentleness. It was the soothing but encouraging words that he whispered in her ears. It was the eager caresses with which he showered her. It was the adulation in his eyes as they poured over her naked body.

It was not only the first time that Erica had felt truly cherished, but it was the first time in her life that she hadn't experienced a need to hide—to camouflage those areas of her body that she felt were imperfect. She knew in her heart that Alex simply didn't see them. To him, she was perfection.

"Let me touch you," she murmured throatily as she stripped his shirt off him and explored every inch of his muscled chest and arms with her hands and her lips, and when she knew that portion of him more intimately than she knew herself, she released his belt and began to explore the rest of him.

"My God, Erica!" Alex exclaimed in a hoarse rasp when she knelt in front of him and stroked him boldly. No woman, not even Kristen, had touched him so wantonly, and when she raised her passion-glazed eyes to his, Alex's heart began to pound with unfulfilled need. Her desire for him touched him in places he'd never even known existed—made him feel as if he could conquer the world.

But it wasn't the world he wanted to conquer. In fact, conquest wasn't even on his mind. He wanted to satisfy Erica. He wanted to touch her in ways no man had ever touched her. He wanted to be special—unique. He *had* to be special for her, because he wanted to be the last thing on her mind when she closed her eyes tonight, and the first thing on it when she awoke tomorrow.

"I don't think God has anything to do with this," she murmured with a husky laugh as she continued to gaze up at him.

"Siren!" he accused as he came to his knees, levered her down to the floor and came over her. "We should be doing this in bed."

"That's so passé. Anyone can do it in a bed."

He tangled his hands in her hair. "We aren't anyone. You do know that, don't you?"

She nodded.

"Say it," he demanded.

"We aren't anyone."

"What do you want?"

"You. I want you inside me, Alex. I want you to take me to that place between heaven and hell. I... want... you."

"Oh, damn, I've gone down for the count," he muttered as he fumbled his wallet out of his pants. "I've gone down for the count, and it's all your fault."

She caught his face between her hands and stared into his eyes steadily. "We can stop now if you don't feel you're ready for this."

"We're not going to stop," he stated adamantly. Silently he added, *We aren't going to stop until you're mine. And you're going to be mine. You're going to belong to me—mind, body and soul.*

"Alex?" Erica whispered uncertainly as she stared up into his unyielding face, but her uncertainty was wiped away as he caught her lips in a possessive kiss that seered and claimed.

Somehow during that kiss, Alex managed to handle the foil packet, and Erica gasped when he surged into her. But it wasn't from pain. It was from the fulfillment he made her feel. It was for the *rightness* that washed through her. She wanted to hold on to that feeling and explore the wonder of it, but Alex began to move inside her with such urgency that need took control and rendered her mindless of anything but the man in her arms.

"Alex!" she cried out in her passion as she arched toward him.

"That's it," he whispered as he rained her face with kisses. "That's it, my sweet. Wrap those long legs around me and hold on tight. Do it. Do it *now*!"

Erica did exactly as he instructed. She wrapped her legs around him and held on tight. Her nails were embedded in his back when he brought her to a climax and he immediately followed her.

She didn't know how much time had passed when he finally rolled to his side and brought her with him. "Are you all right?" he whispered hoarsely.

Erica nodded. "I may have a few rug burns, but the pain hasn't set in yet."

He caught her chin and raised her face to his. "I didn't mean to hurt you."

She would have laughed if he hadn't looked so sincere. Instead she touched his face, loving the scratchy feeling of his evening beard. "Any hurt I felt, you took away, and any hurt I feel later will be worth it."

He pulled her over him. "Feel free to exact your revenge. I won't complain."

"Alex!" she said in amazement when she felt him stirring against her. "You're too old for this."

"I know," he murmured as he kissed her, and then kissed her again. "But I won't tell if you won't."

"It'll be our little secret," she promised with a Siren's laugh.

9

"WHAT ARE YOU DOING?" Alex asked when he opened his eyes and saw Erica sitting cross-legged beside him on the bed. She was wearing an old and frayed terry-cloth robe, her eyes were still heavy from sleep and her hair was in wild disarray. He'd never seen a woman look so gorgeous.

She grinned. "I was watching you sleep. You look as innocent as Josh, and the sweetest little smile curves your lips."

Alex arched an admonishing brow. "Men don't have sweet smiles, Erica."

"You do, but don't worry about it. Your secret's safe with me."

"You're incorrigible," he said with a laugh as he caught her hand and pulled her down to his chest. He tugged her robe open and swept his hands over her. "And so incredibly soft."

"Mmm," she hummed contentedly as she pressed her lips against his shoulder. "So are you."

"Men aren't soft, either. They're hard."

She smiled devilishly. "Only sometimes."

He heaved a mock-aggrieved sigh. "What am I going to do with you?"

"Well, if you're asking for suggestions..." she murmured coquettishly as she threaded her fingers through the mat of hair on his chest.

Alex tenderly brushed her tangled hair away from her face. "As much as I'd like to take you up on that offer, I'm afraid I'm out of protection. I'll have to take a rain check."

"No, you won't," Erica replied as she levered herself over him and opened the drawer of her bedside table. She hauled out a box and waved it in front of his face.

"Where in hell did you get those?" Alex demanded as he sat up, sending Erica sprawling.

Erica gazed up at him in wide-eyed amazement. He was furious! "They were a gift. Why?"

"A gift?" he bellowed. He grabbed the box out of her hand and shook it at her. "What kind of a man gives a woman a gift like this?"

"Why, Alex, you're jealous!" she exclaimed in glee.

He glowered at her."I am not jealous. I'm . . ."

"Jealous," she repeated smugly as she sat up and grinned at him. "Come on, Alex. 'Fess up. It's not a crime, you know. In fact, I think it's probably a pretty healthy sign."

"Erica, don't push me," he muttered from between clenched teeth. "Right now I'm so angry with you that I want to turn you over my knee."

"Because you think there's been another man in my life?" she asked cheerfully, nonplussed by the threat. Before he could respond, she said, "There hasn't been, Alex, although I will admit that it hasn't been due to a lack of opportunity. Just personal preference."

"Then how do you explain these?" he asked, waving the box at her again.

"When my divorce was final, some of my girlfriends threw me a freedom party. They gave me gifts that they felt every single woman should have on hand. That was one of them." She gave him a wicked smile. "They also gave me this little black nightie with peek-a-boo holes that . . ."

"Damn you," he muttered as he tossed the box aside and hauled her into his arms.

"Was that supposed to be a sweet nothing to be whispered in my ear?" she asked, smiling up at him sweetly. "If it was, Alex, you need to work on the delivery. The growl just doesn't incite a romantic mood."

"If you want romance, then I'll give you romance," he said as he tugged her robe off her. When she was naked in his arms, his eyes poured over her. "You're gorgeous."

Erica shivered in pleasure at his words. "I don't know, Alex. I'm pretty small up top, I have stretch marks and my hips are definitely leaning toward secretarial spread."

"Hmm. Well, maybe I'd better check these imperfections out."

"Maybe you'd better!" Erica gasped as he lowered his head to her breast.

"Nope. Not too small. Just the right size," he murmured as he laved his tongue over her nipple, bringing it to turgid attention. "The same here," he mumbled when he moved to her other breast.

"Alex, stop torturing me," she whispered hoarsely when he lowered her to the mattress and slowly trailed his lips down to her abdomen.

He ignored her words as he pressed a wet kiss to each of the five stretch marks that she'd earned through pregnancy. "These are so sexy," he said. He splayed his hand across her stomach and raised his head. His eyes were glowing with hot passion, turning Erica's insides to molten lava. "I wish I could have seen you pregnant. What did it feel like?"

She shook her head, at a loss for words. "I don't know how to describe it. It was the most incredible experience I've ever had. It was also the most frightening."

"Why?" he questioned as he lay down beside her and drew her into his arms.

"Why was I frightened?" He nodded, and she said, "Because after a certain point, pregnancy is the one thing in your life that you can't change your mind about. You have to go through with it, and no one can do it for you."

He stroked her hip as he stared into her eyes. "Did you have a lot of pain when you gave birth?"

"No more than the average woman, I suppose, but, yes, it was painful."

"Would you go through it again?"

Erica frowned inwardly as she peered at him. Last night he'd told her his ex-wife's feelings regarding motherhood. Was this some type of test? Intuition told her the answer he wanted to hear, but she knew she couldn't give it to him—at least, not in the uncomplicated manner that he was expecting.

"I think that would depend upon a lot of things," she hedged.

His hand tightened on her hip. "What kinds of things?"

"Alex, where is this conversation going?"

When he didn't answer, she raised up on her elbow and eyed him assessingly. However, she couldn't define the emotion in his eyes.

"You were right," he suddenly said, and she blinked in surprise.

"Right about what?"

"I was jealous. I *am* jealous." He tumbled her back down to the mattress and straddled her hips. After placing a hand on either side of her head, he said, "I absolutely hate the fact that you belonged to another man.

That he touched you the way I've touched you. That he's kissed you the way I've kissed you. That he's made love to you the way I've made love to you. That he's given you a son."

His brow creased with a contemplative frown. "What do you think it all means?"

"That you're human?" Erica suggested. "I'm jealous, too. I wonder how many woman you've touched the way you've touched me. How many you've kissed the way you've kissed me. How many you've made love to the way you've made love to me."

When he parted his lips to speak, she laid a finger against his lips. "Don't answer those questions, because I don't really want an answer. The past is over with and done. We couldn't change it if we wanted to. What we need to do is concentrate on the present—on *us*." She gave him a come-hither smile and said provocatively, "And I know exactly how I'd like to start that concentration."

He grinned as he rocked back on his knees and settled his hands on her hips. "You were right, again. You are definitely heading in the direction of secretarial spread," he teased.

"Alex!"

"It's okay," he crooned as he leaned down and kissed her. "It just gives me more of you to love. Now, about that black nightie with the peek-a-boo holes..."

"MY WORD, ERICA, if you get any more dreamy-eyed, I'm going to get sick to my stomach," Laura told her as she measured out laundry soap and dumped it into her washer.

"Sorry," Erica said without one ounce of remorse. She flashed her friend an impish grin. "What were you saying?"

"It doesn't matter," Laura grumbled. She started the washer and sat down at the kitchen table. "What does matter is you. Just what are Alex's intentions?"

"Wicked, I hope," Erica answered with a teasing leer. "Why?"

Laura drummed her fingers against the tabletop. "When I encouraged you to see the man, I didn't mean that you should jump into it with such . . ."

"Vigor?" Erica offered. She perched her elbows on the table and rested her chin in her hands. "He's wonderful, Laura, and I mean *wonderful*!"

Laura groaned. "If this is a taste of what I have to look forward to when my kids discover sex, I'm giving them up for adoption the moment they hit puberty. Will you please take your head out of the clouds long enough to look at this situation sensibly?"

"Sure," Erica said. "What sensibility am I supposed to look at?"

"Motivation," Laura answered. "Yours and his."

"I think our motivation is fairly clear-cut. I want him and he wants me. He also likes Josh, and Josh likes him. What more could I ask for?"

"I give up," Laura said, throwing her hands into the air in exasperation. Then she said, "No, I don't give up. You're my friend, and I'm obligated to make you take off those rose-colored glasses. I'm concerned about you, Erica. Mark has you in such a tailspin that I don't think you know your own mind. And has it occurred to you that Alex may be playing on that? Have you asked yourself if he could be using you so you'll go to contract on the other three commercials?"

"As a matter of fact, I have," Erica admitted.

"And what answer did you come up with?"

"I didn't come up with one," Erica stated honestly. "But I guess I'll soon find out, because if Josh does as well on the next couple of shoots as he did yesterday, I'm going to go to contract on the remainder of the commercials. I need the money to fight Mark, and I need it doubly bad after yesterday's revelation that he flatly refuses to settle out of court."

"You don't have to go to contract on the other commercials if you don't want to," Laura interjected quickly. "Bob and I talked it over, and we'll loan you the money."

Erica slumped back in her chair. "Thank you for offering, but I couldn't take your money."

"You wouldn't be taking it. It would be a loan. It would also give you an opportunity to find out the truth about Alex before you get in any deeper. At least think about it, Erica. I don't want to see you get hurt."

"I don't want to see me get hurt, either," Erica said as she drew an imaginary figure eight on the table with the tip of her finger. When she was finished, she raised her gaze to her friend's concerned face. "But I have to place my trust in Alex, Laura, because I think I'm falling in love with him."

"That's what I was afraid of," Laura said with a resigned sigh.

"BOOM!" JOSH YELLED.

"You sunk me," Alex said as he pushed the toy battleship to the bottom of the bathtub. "I guess this means the war is over, and since the water is getting cold, it's time for you to get out of the tub, sport."

"But I don't want to," Josh automatically said.

Alex grinned at him as he unplugged the drain. "I think you use those five little words all the time because you know they drive your mother nuts. But I've got you figured out, kid. You're all talk and no action." He lifted Josh out of the tub, stood him on the bath mat and reached for the towel.

Josh took off running toward the open door, yelling, "Catch me!"

"Josh, come back here," Alex ordered. "You mother will shoot me if she finds you running through the house dripping wet and buck naked."

Josh giggled as he glanced over his shoulder, and then headed down the hallway.

Alex chuckled and shook his head. During the past week he'd discovered that the child was definitely a handful, but it was good, wholesome mischief. He caught up with Josh in the living room, snagged the towel around him and lifted him off his feet at the same time.

Josh was laughing in uproarish pleasure, and he threw his arms around Alex's neck. He pressed an exuberant kiss to Alex's cheek before announcing, "I love you."

Alex had to swallow hard against the sudden lump in his throat. "Yeah, well, I love you, too," he muttered gruffly. "Even if you are dripping wet and..."

"Buck naked," Josh finished for him.

Alex cursed inwardly. Erica kept telling him to watch what he said because Josh repeated everything he heard, and he had a feeling that she wasn't going to be pleased with this new addition to her son's vocabulary.

He decided, however, that if he made a production over the words, it would only encourage the kid to use them, so he said, "Let's get you into your pajamas and then we'll go drag your mother out of the garage. I think she's worked enough for tonight, don't you?"

Josh nodded.

Alex had just started for Josh's bedroom when the doorbell rang, and he switched directions. When he opened the door, he didn't have to be told who the man was standing on the doorstep. He was a grown-up version of the toddler in his arms.

Mark Stewart looked momentarily startled by Alex's presence, but he quickly recovered and extended his hand. "I'm Mark Stewart. Josh's father."

Alex reluctantly accepted the man's hand. "Alex Harte."

"Is Erica around?" Mark asked.

"She's in the garage working. If you'll come in, I'll get her as soon as I get Josh into his pajamas."

"Oh, I think I can put Josh into his pajamas," he said. He held his arms out to Josh. "Come here and give me a hug."

"No," Josh said belligerently, tightening his hold around Alex's neck until he was practically strangling him.

"He's in one of his contrary moods. A stage, you know," Alex explained, knowing that he should be encouraging the boy to go to his father, but unable to bring himself to do so.

"I keep telling Erica that she's too lenient with him," Mark replied. "That old saying, 'Spare the rod and spoil the child' is true. A child needs discipline. If they don't get it early on, they become impossible to handle when they're older."

Alex saw red, but he forced the haze away. He also managed to withhold comment. Getting into a verbal battle with Erica's ex-husband over his views on discipline would only make a tense situation more tense.

"Well, if you'll excuse me, I'll get Josh into his pajamas." He walked away, leaving Mark standing in the open doorway.

"I don't like him. He's not nice," Josh said when Alex carried him into his room.

"My sentiments exactly," Alex muttered beneath his breath.

He nearly had Josh dressed when the back door slammed and Erica called out, "Josh? Alex? Where are you?" Before he could respond, he heard her say, "What are *you* doing here?" Mark's response was muffled, but Erica's vehement "No!" was loud and clear.

"I think, sport, that you'd better play in here for a little while," Alex told Josh as he snapped the last snap on his pajamas.

"Mama's mad," Josh said, scrambling off the bed and heading for his toy box as Erica began to yell and Mark Stewart's voice raised, as well. They were screaming so loudly that Alex couldn't make out one word of the conversation.

"What's the problem?" he asked when he walked into the living room during a lull. Erica was standing in front of Mark, her hands clenched into fists and her body trembling with rage.

Mark glanced toward him, his face a mask of fury. "This is a private conversation."

Alex leaned against the wall and casually crossed his arms over his chest. "At the volume it's being conducted, I'd say it's fairly public. However, if Erica wants me to make myself scarce, I'll be happy to do so. Erica?"

She pivoted her head toward him. "You're not going anywhere, Alex. If anyone if going to make themselves scarce, it's Mark." She turned back to her ex-usband. "Get out, Mark, and take your filthy proposition with you. My son is not for sale."

"That's your problem, Erica," Mark sneered. "You refuse to face facts. Josh is my son, too, and I'm going to win if we go into court. Just make it easy on yourself for once and take the money, because I can guarantee that I won't make the offer again."

"You'll get your hands on Josh over my dead body," she railed. "You don't care about him. You've never cared about him. All you want is to get your revenge against me for walking out on you and bruising your damned ego."

"You're just as delusional as ever," he drawled, his lips curving into a demeaning smile. "It takes a woman to bruise a man's ego, and we both know that you aren't a woman. If you were, I wouldn't have had to seek my pleasures elsewhere, would I?"

Erica didn't even realize she was going to slap him until her hand connected with his face. Pain shot from her palm down to her elbow and she leaped backward, bringing her hand to her mouth in horror. She'd never struck anyone in anger, and the fact that Mark had managed to lower her to such a base level brought tears of humiliation to her eyes.

When he reached for her, she couldn't even move, but he stopped abruptly when Alex stated softly, dangerously, "If you want to keep your arm attached to your body, then you'd better not touch her."

Mark was so livid that his eyes were bulging, but when he glanced toward Alex, he apparently decided that retreat was the watchword in this instance.

"I'll see you in court," he stated tightly. "Bring Josh's bags with you, because he won't set foot back in this house." With that, he pivoted on his heel and slammed out the front door.

"I can't believe I hit him," Erica mumbled as she stared at the door. "I can't believe I did it."

"He asked for it, Erica," Alex said as he came up behind her and drew her back against him. "What he said to you was unnecessarily cruel."

"That's no excuse for what I did," she said, resting her head against his chest and releasing a weary sigh. "It isn't the first time he's placed the blame on me for his infidelities, but I know it isn't true. So why did I get so angry?"

Alex turned her in his arms, caught her chin and raised her head so he could look into her eyes. "I'd venture to say that it's because you've been storing up a lot of anger. You had to erupt eventually, and Mark just happened to push the right button tonight."

He paused, reluctant to ask the next question, but knowing he had to. "Did I understand him right? Did he offer you money for Josh?"

"Yes," Erica replied with a bitter laugh. "In fact, he offered me a fortune. I was so incensed that I wanted to claw his eyes out, but in retrospect, I don't know why I didn't expect it. Mark Stewart has always used his money to get what he wanted. It was only a matter of time before he tried to use it to get Josh."

Alex chewed on his lip thoughtfully. "Mark Stewart. Are we talking about the heir to Stewart Arms?" he hazarded, knowing the name had sounded familiar but he hadn't been able to place it until now.

"One and the same."

"Damn, you are up against some big guns, aren't you? No pun intended."

"Don't remind me," Erica muttered as she rested her head against his chest. "Just hold me, Alex, and tell me it's going to be all right."

Alex tangled his fingers in her short cap of enchanting curls and held her close, wishing he could say the words she wanted him to say, but he couldn't bring himself to lie to her. She wasn't a fool, and they both knew it. Justice was supposed to be blind, but the truth was, money talked, and Mark Stewart had enough wealth to sway the scales of justice a hundred times over.

Just the thought that the man might win his custody suit made Alex ill. Josh was one of the most well-adjusted children he'd ever run across. He was full of life and love. What would happen to him if he was taken away from his mother? Alex didn't even want to consider that possibility, especially when he recalled Josh's unabashed declaration of love for him tonight. Alex knew it was dangerous, but for a moment there, he'd begun to think of Josh as his own son.

"So what did you think of my ex-husband?" Erica eventually asked.

Alex grinned. "Josh summed him up perfectly. I think his exact words were, 'I don't like him. He's not nice.'"

Erica burst into laughter and looped her arms around his neck. "He's an eloquent little devil, isn't he?"

"He sure is," he agreed as he wrapped his arms around her waist and rocked her from side to side. "And speaking of eloquent, I think I should confess that I inadvertently introduced some new words into his vocabulary this evening. What's your reaction to buck naked?"

"Buck naked?" she repeated softly as she slid her hand down his back and caressed his tight buttocks. "I'll be happy to give you my reaction the minute Josh has fallen asleep."

"Where's the sandman when you need him?" Alex asked as he treated her to an ardent kiss.

ALEX HAD FALLEN INTO A DOZE, and Erica crept out of bed, pulled on her robe and went into the living room. The scene with Mark had upset her more than she wanted to admit. It had also brought all her doubts about Alex to the forefront. She'd known for a week now that she was going to go ahead with the rest of the commercials, but she hadn't been able to find the courage to tell him. What if Laura was right? What if he was using sex to get her to bend to his will?

But even as she asked herself that question, she dismissed it. Tonight was only the second time they'd made love, and he'd been at the house nearly every night for a week.

No, he wasn't using sex, she decided, but she feared that he might be using an even more seductive technique. When he was with her and Josh, he created the illusion that they were a family.

Erica settled on the sofa and reached for her sketchpad. When she'd finished pouring all of her agitation onto paper, she studied the monster with a critical eye. It portrayed all the emotions swirling through her—feelings of anger, betrayal, confusion and fear. What she had to do now was find a way to untwist them so she could determine which of them were merely brought on by her insecurities.

"I knew you were upset," Alex stated, startling her as he confiscated her sketchpad. He studied it with a frown. "Monster Woman strikes again."

He settled down beside her, tossed the sketchpad aside, pulled her feet into his lap and began to massage them. Erica found herself automatically relaxing beneath the soothing action, and he caught her off guard when he asked, "How old were you when you started drawing monsters to release your hostility?"

Uneasy with his perceptiveness, Erica tried to pull her feet away from him so she could curl up into a protective ball. He caught her ankles, however, and held them in place as he stared at her compellingly. He didn't say another word, but Erica knew he was asking her to trust him.

It was the most difficult emotional step Erica had taken in her life, but she forced herself to relax. As she'd told Laura, she thought she was falling in love with him, and love and trust had to walk hand in hand.

"I began to draw monsters when I was ten," she answered. When Alex didn't respond but returned to his massage, she continued with, "That was the year I started growing up. I landed fewer and fewer modeling jobs, and eventually they dried up completely. All my life my mother had declared that I was going to be the next Shirley Temple, and it was bad enough that she had to face the fact that I couldn't act my way out of a paper bag, but she suddenly had an ugly duckling on her hands."

"*That's* why you reacted so badly last week to Ron's comment about Josh being a male Shirley Temple," Alex stated softly.

"Yeah." Erica tunneled her hands through her hair. "The more impossible my mother became, the more my father came to my defense. They fought constantly, and I was always at the center of their battles. I felt so guilty about growing up and causing such dissension, and one day I just poured all those feelings out on paper. My counselor says it's therapeutic, and I have to agree with her."

Alex dropped her feet to the floor, caught her hand and drew her to his side. When he had her cuddled in the crook of his arm, he pressed a kiss to the top of her head.

"I used to blame my mother, but I've learned to understand her motivation," Erica continued with a sigh. "She grew up in poverty, and she has a terrible fear of being poor. She didn't have much of an education, and she's insecure in her own abilities. She was simply trying to live her life vicariously through me. Inside, she's a very vulnerable woman, Alex. She just keeps it hidden so well that I tend to forget that."

"I can understand now why you were so adamantly opposed to Josh doing the commercials," he said.

Erica instinctively stiffened, waiting for him to pursue the subject. After all, she'd just given him the perfect opening.

To her surprise, however, all he said was, "I hate to make love and run, but after your run-in with Mark this evening, I don't think it would be wise for me to spend the night. I don't want to give him any ammunition to use against you."

Erica released a short, mirthless laugh. "Considering Mark's extramarital escapades, I don't think he'd be foolish enough to open up the issue of sex. That would really be a Pandora's box for him."

"Still, I'm not going to take the chance." Alex reluctantly eased her away from him. He was worried about her, and he didn't want to leave, which, quite frankly, scared the hell out of him. The more time he spent with her and Josh, the more he wanted to be with them. If he wasn't careful, he'd find himself falling in love, and he wasn't certain if he'd be falling in love with them or the sense of family he experienced when he was with them.

Erica followed him back to the bedroom and sat on her bed, watching him while he finished dressing. A part of her wanted to pull his clothes back off and drag him to bed, but another part said it was time for her to lay her cards on the table. Tonight she'd revealed too many intimate parts of herself to him, and now she had to know if she'd made the right choice.

When she walked him to the front door, he caught her face in his hands and gave her a hard kiss. "If you need me for anything, and I mean *anything*, Erica, even if it's just to talk, call me."

"Thanks," she said.

"I mean it. There are other options besides monsters to ease stress."

She smiled. "I know. You gave me a good example of that tonight."

"Don't look at me like that," he stated gruffly. "It's too tempting."

"Go," she said with a soft laugh as she opened the door and pushed him out. He was half-way across the lawn when she said, "Alex?"

"Yeah?" he said as he turned around to face her.

"I've decided to let Josh do the rest of the commercials. If you can get the contract ready tomorrow, I'll sign it after the shoot."

With that she closed the door, leaving Alex standing in the middle of her yard with his mouth gaping in dumbfounded disbelief.

"Well, tomorrow, we should have some answers," she said to Kitty, who wandered into the room and began to rub against her ankles. "I just hope they're the ones I want."

She picked up the cat and carried it to bed. It wouldn't be the same as having Alex sleeping beside her, but at least it would be a warm body.

10

ERICA REFUSED TO ASK about Alex when she arrived at the studio and he wasn't there. It certainly wasn't the first time he'd arrived after they had, but the fear she'd been battling all night only became more intense. She'd given him what he wanted, and now he had no reason to pursue her.

Josh had just finished with wardrobe and makeup when Ron walked into the studio and said, "Hi, Erica. I just hung up from Alex. He has an unexpected appointment with a potential client and can't make today's shoot. He said he'd meet you at his office after we're done here."

Erica forced herself to return his smile. "Thanks for the message."

"Sure. So how are you and Kitty today, Josh?" Ron asked.

"Kitty's bad," Josh answered.

"Oh, yeah?" Ron said with a chuckle. "What did Kitty do?"

"She . . . she . . ." He looked to his mother for help.

"She decided that the sofa was a scratching post," Erica muttered disgruntledly.

"Oops." Ron tousled Josh's hair. "Well, Josh, I think you're going to have to work very hard to train Kitty to leave the sofa alone. Are you ready to get started?"

"Uh-huh," Josh said as he scrambled down off the chair he was sitting on, grabbed his kitten off the floor and headed for the set. "Let's go."

"I wish I had as much enthusiasm for my work," Ron told Erica wryly.

"Me, too," Erica answered, wishing she'd had the foresight to bring along her sketchpad so she could get all of her frustrations down on paper. She had a feeling that it was going to be a very long two hours.

By the time the shoot was over, she'd worked herself into a dither. A part of her kept insisting that she had to take Alex's excuse for being absent at face value, but the other part kept portending doom.

Why had she let herself walk into his trap? Why had she told him so much about herself? Why, oh why, had she let herself fall in love? And she knew it was love. If it wasn't, she wouldn't hurt so badly right now.

All the way to Alex's office she kept telling herself that she could handle this. She could be all business. She would be cool, calm and collected and pretend that she and Alex had never shared more than a conversation about the weather.

Who was she trying to fool? If she didn't end up bursting into tears, she'd probably end up screaming at him. Damn Alexander Harte! She wasn't going to let him have the upper hand. She was strong. She could handle anything life threw at her, including a hotshot advertising executive without a conscience.

When she strode into his office, she was ready for battle.

ALEX'S MEETING had run much later than he'd anticipated, and he knew that Erica was probably pacing the floors. He shouldn't have stopped at the toy store, he told himself, but when he'd walked by it he hadn't been able to ignore its lure.

He gave the bag in his hand a shake, feeling a rush of excitement. Today he was going to get to do something he'd wanted to do all of his life.

When he walked into his receptionist's office, however, his excitement died. Erica was sitting with her legs crossed, one foot swinging impatiently and her arms folded over her chest militantly. If her posture hadn't told him she was furious, the deadly look in her eyes was a sure giveaway.

Alex felt a momentary pang of guilt, but then his temper began to stir. He knew he'd kept her waiting for close to an hour, but it couldn't be helped. He was building a business, and My Fair Baby had begun to leak the word that they were more than satisfied with his campaign. Today's meeting had been nothing more than an impromptu "get to know you" session with the board of directors of an international electronics firm, but he knew deep in his gut that they'd been impressed. If Erica couldn't understand this part of his life, then he was wasting his time on her.

"Good afternoon, Erica. I'm sorry I'm late," he stated with the same formality he'd use to greet a passing stranger.

The cool manner in which he spoke to her pierced Erica's heart with the force of a knife. She'd been right. She'd agreed to the commercials, and Alex had washed his hands of her.

Pride raised its head, and for a moment, she actually considered gathering Josh, who was entertaining Alex's receptionist and secretary, and telling Alex she'd changed her mind. But thankfully, common sense surfaced before she could utter the words. Josh was what was important here, not her pride.

She rose to her feet. "Your apology is accepted. I hope the contract is ready, because I have a lot of work to do, and I can't afford to waste any more time."

She sounded so cold that her words washed over Alex like an Arctic wind. For a moment, he considered dragging her into his arms and kissing her in an effort to chase the chill away, but pride stopped him. If she wanted to be all business, then they'd be all business.

"The contract's on my desk."

"Fine. Josh, come here."

"But I don't want to," he stated adamantly as he plopped down on the floor and stared at his mother in challenge.

Erica ground her teeth and decided that she'd remove that sentence from his conversation if she had to tape his mouth closed.

Before she could insist that he obey her, however, Alex's secretary, Pamela, said, "Janet and I will be happy to watch him, Erica. We love kids. If we didn't, we wouldn't have six of them between us."

"If you're sure you don't mind," Erica relented, deciding that a show of authority with Josh right now would only delay her, and she wanted to put as much distance as possible between her and Alex as soon as possible.

"We don't mind," Janet assured.

"Now that that's settled, my office is this way," Alex stated, leading the way.

When he opened his door and stepped back, Erica entered. She was making a beeline for the chair in front of his desk when he suddenly grabbed her arm and spun her around to face him.

"What is going on?" Alex demanded, deciding to hell with pride. When he'd left her last night, she'd been looking at him as if she could eat him up. Now she was looking at him as if she wanted to chew him up.

"You tell me," Erica answered, her temper taking control. Too hell with being cool, calm and collected. She wanted a fight, and by damn, she was going to get one. "And don't spare me, Alex. Lay it all on the line. I'm tougher than I look, and I can take it."

"What am I supposed to lay on the line?" he bellowed in frustration.

"The truth about today!" she bellowed back.

"I had an appointment. It ran later than I thought it would. I'm sorry I was late, but it couldn't be helped." When she didn't respond, he said, "Okay, maybe I shouldn't have stopped at the toy store, but I was only there for ten minutes. I didn't think it was going to start World War III!"

"You stopped at the toy store?" she asked, staring at him in bemusement, her anger suddenly gone.

"Yeah," he said, shifting from one foot to the other as he experienced a strange flood of embarrassment.

She reached out and touched the bag in his hand. "What did you buy?"

"You'll probably think it's silly."

"I won't know that until you show me what it is."

He walked to his desk and dumped the contents on top of it. Erica found herself staring at two sizes of baseball mitts.

"I got a mitt for me and one for Josh," Alex told her. "I thought I'd call the deli down the street, have them pack us a picnic and we could eat dinner at the small ballpark down the street from your house. Then I thought I could start teaching Josh how to play catch."

Erica's heart lurched as she stared at his face. There was so much vulnerability reflected on it that she wanted to sit down and cry.

"I think Josh would like that," she whispered, her voice trembling.

Alex reached down and ran his hand over one of the mitts. "When I was a kid, I used to envy all the other kids who played catch with their dads. My mom tried to teach me, but she wasn't very good. And the truth is, it wasn't quite the same as having a man throw you a ball."

"Oh, Alex," Erica said as she rounded his desk and settled herself in his arms.

"Hey, it's nothing to cry about," he murmured when he caught a tear rolling down her cheek.

"I thought that since I had agreed to let Josh do the commercials, you didn't want to see me anymore," Erica confessed.

"You what?" he exclaimed in disbelief.

"You heard me."

"Erica, what am I going to do with you?" he asked with a sigh as he hugged her close. "The commercials don't have anything to do with us. I thought you realized that."

"I didn't."

"Well, you do now. What do you think about my proposition? How does a picnic at the ballpark strike you?"

"It sounds great. I should, however, warn you that Josh is very cognizant about the difference between small and big, and as far as he's concerned, big is always better. You might have a little trouble convincing him that he shouldn't be using your mitt."

"I think I can handle that. Now, how about if we kiss and make up?"

Erica eagerly complied with his suggestion.

"I DON'T THINK I've ever seen you look this contented, Erica," her mother said as she helped Erica load dishes into the dishwasher.

"What's not to be contented about?" Erica asked, listening to Josh's and Alex's voices drift in from the backyard. Since Alex had introduced Josh to the game of catch, the boy had hardly given him a moment's peace. Thankfully, Alex didn't seem to mind, and actually seemed to enjoy it.

"Is it serious between you and Alex?" Madelaine asked.

Erica shrugged. "I don't really know, Mother. We've barely been dating a month. I suppose time will give us an answer."

"I've always been skeptical of stepparents," Madelaine said. "But after seeing Alex with Josh, I think Alex is exactly what Josh needs. He's blossoming beneath his attention."

"Alex has been good for Josh," Erica concurred.

Madelaine settled at the table and studied Erica for a long moment before she said, "Have you given any thought to enrolling Josh in acting lessons? He is good, Erica, and you know he is."

Erica shot her mother a resolved look. "I suppose you've lined up half a dozen schools that would take him in at a moment's notice."

"No, I haven't," Madelaine replied. When Erica stared at her disbelievingly, Madelaine gave a firm shake of her head. "I've been tempted, but I haven't done it.

"I know you hate me, Erica," she continued, "and you probably have every reason to feel that way. But I never meant to hurt you. I really do love you, and I always have. It's just that I have this little demon inside me that tends to take control. After your father died, I took a long look at myself in the mirror, and I decided that I didn't like what I saw. I've tried to be better, and I will admit that I've slid back a time or two, but I do understand that Josh is your son, and I'll go along with whatever you decide for him."

Erica leaned against the kitchen counter and regarded Madelaine in amazement. She never would have believed she'd hear those words from her mother. The very fact that Madelaine would even acknowledge that Josh was Erica's son and, as such, was her responsibility was mind-boggling. Maybe there was hope for them yet.

"Actually, once the problem with Mark is resolved, I am thinking about enrolling Josh in acting lessons," Erica said. At her mother's excited smile, Erica quickly inserted, "But I don't plan on auditioning him, Mother. I just want to give him an opportunity to explore his talent. He has his entire life ahead of him, and I want him to be able to pick and choose from a wide variety of careers. If acting is what he wants, then I'll support him. But if it isn't, I'll support him in that, too."

If Madelaine was disappointed, she didn't show it. "Well, at least you'll be giving him a chance. Now, what can I do to help with dessert?"

ALEX SAT IN ERICA'S living room and rolled his wineglass between his hands. She was settling Josh down for the night, and he'd already said his good-nights to the boy.

He knew he should feel content, but the truth was, he'd never felt more unsettled. He adored Josh, and he didn't mind having him around. In fact, he loved having him around. But his feelings for Josh were too jumbled up with his feelings for Erica. He couldn't decide if he cared for Josh because of Erica, or Erica because of Josh. Was he falling in love with Erica, or was he falling in love with the life-style she and Josh represented?

What he needed was some time away from them, or better yet, some concentrated time alone with Erica. But with the child-custody hearing for Josh just a few weeks away, he probably had as good a chance of luring Erica away from her son as he had of sprouting wings and flying. So how was he supposed to deal with this dilemma?

"Well, I think he's finally down for the night," Erica announced when she walked into the room and collapsed on the sofa beside him. "And now that Mother's gone, we'll finally have some peace and quiet. How about giving me a sip of your wine?"

Alex passed her the glass and watched her take a sip and savor it. She always seemed to derive such pleasure from anything that passed her lips.

When she handed him back the glass, he downed the remaining liquid and asked, "What are your plans for this weekend?"

Erica, immediately picking up on the strange tone of his voice, pulled her knees up to her chest and shrugged. "I don't have any specific plans. Why?"

"Would you spend the weekend with me? Alone. At my place."

"Why?" she asked again.

Alex pushed himself up off the sofa and walked to the windows. He stared out them for a long time before he finally said, "I'd like us to have some time away from Josh."

"In other words, he's getting on your nerves," Erica murmured in disappointment.

"No," Alex denied as he spun around to face her. "I think Josh is the greatest thing that's come along since chocolate-chip cookies. But I never have any time alone with you, Erica. I can outline every stage that a three-year-old goes through, and I can tell you what to do about it—or at least what *you* would do about it. I can't, however, tell you what your religious preferences are, your political convictions, or even what your favorite color is. Do you know that if I stopped at a florist's shop tomorrow, I wouldn't even know what kind of flowers to buy you? All I really know about you is that you love your son with all your heart."

"If you want to know those things, then all you have to do is ask," Erica rebutted. "My religious preferences are Unitarian. My political preferences are independent. My favorite color is green, and I love carnations in every color, shape and size. What else would you like to know?"

"How you look in an evening dress. How you waltz. How you look across a candlelit table. I want to know all the romantic details, Erica, and I don't want them told to me. I want to experience them. I want to court you, and I can't do that with Josh underfoot."

"I told you in the beginning that Josh and I came as a package deal," she stated tightly.

"Yes, you did, and I understand that," Alex responded fervently. "I'm not asking you to shove Josh aside. I'm asking you to give us one weekend. I want to sweep you out of here on Friday night and take you to dinner in your Sunday best. I want to seduce you over a candlelit table and on a dance floor. I want to take you home and make love with you all night in front of a fire with Rachmaninoff, Tchaikovsky and Debussy playing in the background. I want to cook you my cheese omelet the next morning. I want to read you my favorite poetry, feed you with my fingers, and the list goes on and on and on."

Erica wrapped her arms more tightly around her knees. She knew what he was saying, and just hearing him say it made her yearn for the same thing. But even as her heart begged her for the romantic interlude, her mind reminded her of the deadline she had to meet, of the laundry that had to be done, of the new shoes that Josh needed, and that list went on and on and on.

There was also that tiny little pinprick of doubt deep in her soul that said her days with Josh could be numbered, and she didn't know if she could live with herself if she gave up two of those days just to be wined, dined and seduced by Alex.

But just when she'd decided to tell Alex no she looked at him, and as she stared at his beloved face, she knew that she couldn't live with herself if she didn't give him the time he was asking for. She was in love with him, and she honestly believed that he was falling in love with her. At some point, she had to show him just how much she cared for him, and that meant that she was going to have to place his needs before Josh's and her own.

"All right, Alex. I'll ask Mother to take Josh for the weekend."

"You won't regret it. I promise," he said as he walked to her and pulled her up into his arms.

Neither would he, Erica vowed to herself.

ALEX STEPPED OUT of his car and nervously ran his finger inside the neck of his shirt. He kept telling himself that it was ridiculous to feel like a teenage boy on his first date, but that's exactly how he felt, and he rubbed his damp palms against his pants before grabbing the huge bouquet of carnations out of the passenger seat. He actually felt tongue-tied as he walked to Erica's door.

But if he'd felt tongue-tied on his way to her door, the moment Erica opened it he was struck dumb. As his gaze traveled from the top of her coiffed head, over the strapless, black sheath clinging to her curves, down her shapely black-silk stockinged legs, to her spike-heeled black sandals, he wondered how he could have ever thought that she wasn't a femme fatale.

She ran one arm up the door frame, cocked a hip and rested her hand on it in a seductive pose. Alex nearly choked when he saw the slit that went from her knee almost to her hip, and the black garter sporting a small red rose that was secured high on her thigh.

"Well, sailor, what do you think?" she drawled in a throaty Mae West imitation.

What he thought was that he needed to strip off his coat and cover her up before anyone else saw her. Good heavens, what were the neighbors going to think?

He cleared his throat. "You're absolutely beautiful, but don't you think that dress is a little, uh, daring for a mother?"

She lazily lifted her hand from her hip and ran her index finger down his cheek, along his jaw and tapped it against his chin. "I'm not a mother this weekend, remember? I'm a woman being courted. Would you like a drink before we go? I have diet cola and orange soda. You finished the wine the other night."

"I'll pass," Alex answered, deciding that what he needed was a hefty belt of Scotch. In fact, make that two belts and a quart to go. If he got enough alcohol in him, it might lower his libido enough to keep him from jumping her the minute her back was turned.

"Are the flowers for me, or is that an extravagant boutonniere?" she asked, a hint of laughter in her voice.

Alex blushed and handed her the flowers. "They're for you."

"They're beautiful," she murmured. She closed her eyes, buried her nose in the flowers and inhaled deeply.

Alex caught his breath and held it until he nearly turned blue, certain she was going to pop right out of her bodice. To his immense relief, she didn't.

"Would you like to come in while I put them in water?" she inquired with a flirtatious bat of her lashes. "It'll only take me a minute."

"No, I think I'd better wait right here," Alex replied, knowing that if he set foot in her house they'd be there for the duration of the weekend, and he was determined to get Erica out of her element and into his. He had to find some answers about his feelings for her, even if she did have him as hot as a volcano preparing for eruption.

"Suit yourself," she said, pivoting on her three-inch heels so gracefully that she could have been born in them.

Alex succumbed to a coughing spell as he watched her walk away, the high heels exaggerating the already provocative sway of her hips. It dawned on him that it was going to be one hell of a long night.

"Where's your wrap and your suitcase?" he asked when she returned and slung a small purse attached to a long gold chain over her bare shoulder.

She gave him a bewitching smile and patted her purse. "It's too warm for a wrap, Alex, and everything I need for the weekend is right in here. I think you're going to be very. . . pleased."

Alex nearly lost his control for good. But what had he expected? he grumbled to himself. He'd told her he wanted to experience all the romance, and it looked as if she were throwing herself into the endeavor wholeheartedly. That old saying, "Be careful of what you wish for..." flashed through his mind. It wasn't as if he weren't enjoying this. He just would have been able to enjoy it a whole lot more if he didn't have to look forward to glowering at every man they ran into tonight.

He helped her into his car and then joined her, discovering that her perfume had filled the interior in those few brief seconds. It was alluring enough to blow the top of a man's head off, not to mention the physical damage it could do to him elsewhere.

"Is that a new perfume?" he asked hoarsely as he ineffectually tried to put the key into the ignition.

"Yes." Erica leaned toward him and placed her hand high on his thigh, raking her nails against his pants. "Do you like it?"

"It's very nice," he stated stiffly. "Now, why don't you sit back and buckle up? There is a seat-belt law in this state."

Erica chuckled to herself as she complied with his request. She'd never tried to seduce a man before, but when Alex had claimed that he wanted all the romance, she'd decided to pull out all the stops. Now she was discovering that it was so much fun that she wished he'd pushed the issue weeks before.

She leaned her head back against the seat, closed her eyes and let her mind drift with the soft music coming from the radio. For the next forty-eight hours she wasn't going to let herself think about anything but Alex. She was going to cater to his every whim and a few of her own—boy, was she going to cater to a few of her own! she thought, smiling in self-satisfaction as she patted her purse that contained her black nightie with the peek-a-boo holes.

Alex had managed to regain some of his composure during the drive to the expensive French restaurant he'd chosen for dinner and dancing, but he lost it the moment he began to help Erica out of the car. The split in her skirt opened as she stepped out, displaying enough leg to cause a traffic accident. The red rose on her garter seemed to wink at him.

Alex growled an imprecation beneath his breath when someone in the parking lot let out a long, low wolf whistle.

"What did you say, Alex?" Erica asked, peering up at him in wide-eyed innocence.

"Not a thing," he muttered between clenched teeth, deciding that when tonight was over, he was going to burn the damn dress. She was a mother, for pity's sake, and mothers were *not* supposed to be whistled at in restaurant parking lots.

He took a proprietary hold on her arm and didn't let go until the maitre d' had them seated at their table, which, thankfully, was located in a nice, dark corner.

Erica hid her grin behind her menu as Alex shifted in his chair several times before finally finding a position that seemed comfortable. She slipped off her shoes to get comfortable herself.

When he asked her what she'd like to eat, she gave him her best seductive smile, ran her stockinged foot up his pants leg and crooned, "Something that's heavy on oysters. After all, we do have a long, *long* night ahead of us, and we need to keep up our strength."

Alex jerked his leg away from her marauding foot and exclaimed lowly, "Erica, what in the world has gotten into you?!"

"Nothing yet, but I'm sure you'll take care of that before the night is over," she drawled suggestively.

Alex could only gape at her. What had happened to his nice, sweet, motherly, cookie-baking, monster-drawing Erica, who wiped away Josh's tears and wore that adorable old and frayed terry-cloth bathrobe?

It was then that everything clicked for Alex. He'd been fretting over his feelings for her, unable to decide if it was her he was falling for or the life-style she led. The fact of the matter was, she and her life-style went hand in hand, and if he fell for one, then he automatically fell for the other. It didn't mean that he didn't like this side of her, but he didn't want it displayed in public. He wanted it to come out behind closed doors with the safety latch in place.

"Come on, we're getting out of here," he said as he rose to his feet.

"But, Alex, we haven't had dinner, and... Alex! What are you doing?" she yelped when he suddenly pulled her chair away from the table, dropped her purse into her lap and scooped her up into his arms.

"Alex, my shoes are under the table," she complained mildly, rather enjoying this sudden caveman side of his nature as he carried her toward the door.

"I'll buy you a new pair of shoes. A nice pair of sneakers, I think. If you're good, I might even let you get a pair with a racing stripe, but only one racing stripe, Erica. You are a mother, after all, and mothers are not supposed to be racy."

Erica giggled and said, "Smile and wave, Alex. We're making a scene and everyone is looking."

"It's okay," he stated loudly. "We're just falling in love."

Erica burst into roaring laughter when everyone in the restaurant began to applaud.

11

"I THOUGHT YOU WANTED romance," Erica said when Alex carried her into his apartment and set her on her feet.

"I do," he replied as he closed and locked the door. "I just don't want it out in the open for everyone to see."

"Why, Alex, has anyone ever told you that you have prudish tendencies?" she teased.

"Nope," he said as he turned and gathered her into his arms. "Until now, I've been open-minded and liberal. If a woman wanted to wear her dress open from her neck to her kneecaps, that was fine with me. But you're different. I want you buttoned up from top to toe." He pressed a quick kiss to the end of her nose. "If you're hungry, I'll order us a pizza."

"Oh, I'm hungry, but it isn't for pizza," she murmured as she slid her hands beneath his jacket and leaned against him.

She closed her eyes and sighed in contentment when he nuzzled his nose in her hair and whispered. "What are you hungry for?"

"I'm hungry to make love with you all night in front of a fire with Rachmaninoff, Tchaikovsky and Debussy playing in the background. I'm starving to eat your cheese omelet in the morning. I'm positively ravenous to listen to you read me your favorite poetry, feed me with your fingers, and the list goes on and on and on," she answered.

"Well, with an appetite like that, we'd better get started. It could take us all weekend to get you sated."

"At least all weekend," she agreed as she stood on tiptoe and pressed her lips to his.

Alex had been burning up with need for her before he'd carried her out of the restaurant. But now that he had her here alone, soft and sweet and complacent in his arms, the urgency had disappeared. He turned on the music and lit the fire in the fireplace. Then he led Erica to the pile of pillows in front of it.

He took his time taking off her clothes, stopping to admire the way a moonbeam danced across her cute nose. The soft slope of her shoulders. The upthrust tilt of her breasts. The way her waist dipped and her spine curved in the small of her back. The silken feel of her skin at the back of her knee. The shape of her small toes.

Everything about her filled him with wonder, and he stood back to stare at her when he'd finally completed the task. She looked so delicate and fragile as she stood before him in her glorious nakedness, but he knew that when he touched her, she'd feel strong and warm and vibrant.

"My turn," Erica whispered throatily as she pushed his jacket off his shoulders and began to disrobe him with the same care he'd used with her. When she pulled off his shirt, she explored him with the same wonder as he had her, running her hand up his hair-covered chest, over his shoulder and down his back. He was such a marvelous contrast of textures—rough and smooth, hard and soft. She trembled at the conflicting sensations and pressed her lips to his shoulder.

"You're only half-done," he reminded her, his voice low and gravelly with desire.

"I know, but I want to take my time. I want to memorize every inch of you."

Alex groaned deep in his chest and reached for her, but Erica stepped back quickly, avoiding his hands.

"No touching until you're as naked as I am."

"Then get on with it, because I can't take much more, Erica."

She reached for his belt buckle and his stomach muscles jumped beneath her fingers and then tightened as she took her time undoing his belt. She took even more time lowering his zipper, reveling in the power and heat of his arousal pulsing beneath her touch.

"Erica!" he growled in warning when she slipped her hands inside his slacks and caressed his tight, cotton-covered buttocks.

She dropped to her knees and removed his shoes and socks. Finally she reached up and removed his pants, leaving him wearing only his jockey shorts. She ran her hands up his legs loving the way the hair felt against her palms—the way the muscles trembled beneath her touch. When she hooked her fingers in the elastic at his waist and flicked her tongue across her lips in anticipation, he closed his eyes and sucked in a deep breath.

"Erica, please hurry up. If I can't touch you within the next two seconds, I'm going to explode."

But despite his warning, Erica took her time in revealing the true strength of him—the life of him—and when she'd removed that last scrap of clothing, she could only sit back on her heels and gaze up at him in awe.

"You are so magnificent, Alex. So very, very magnificent."

Alex's heart hesitated as he stared down into her face. Her eyes glowed with desire. Her expression was wanton. He dropped to his knees in front of her, hauled her into his arms and lowered her to the pillows, barely holding on to enough sanity to remember to protect her. They came together with an urgent passion that seared and soothed.

He was in love with her, he admitted as they neared the pinnacle. He was in love with her, and he didn't know what to do about it.

He decided to think about it later when Erica tightened her legs around him, dug her nails into his back and cried out his name in passionate need. Much, much later. He sealed his lips over hers and their bodies shuddered together in release.

ERICA WASN'T SURPRISED when she woke up on Sunday morning and found Alex gone. Ever since they'd made love Friday night, she'd sensed him growing more and more tense. At first she'd thought that he'd decided their weekend together was a mistake, but she'd quickly dismissed that assertion when he pulled her into his arms and kissed her as if she were the most cherished item in the world and had continued to treat her as such the entire weekend. So what in the world was bothering him?

There was only one way to find out, and that was to ask.

She slipped into the soft flannel shirt he'd given her to use as a robe and went looking for him. He was wearing a pair of cutoffs and lay sprawled in a lounge chair on the balcony, staring at the distant view of the ocean.

"Good morning, beautiful," he murmured when she joined him. He caught her hand and leaned her down for a kiss. "What are you doing up so early?"

"Well, I woke up and found your side of the bed empty. I can't warm my feet on cold sheets."

He chuckled as he hooked an arm around her waist and pulled her down to his lap. "Then feel free to warm them up on me."

She curled up against him and tucked her feet between his legs. Several minutes passed before she found the courage to ask, "What's wrong, Alex?"

"Nothing's wrong," he replied easily, but Erica had felt the slight stiffening of his body at her question.

"Alex, we've been too intimate for me not to know when something's bothering you, so please, don't lie to me." She leaned her head back so she could peer up at him. "Have you decided that this weekend was a mistake? That you don't want to see me anymore? If you have, then tell me. I promise that I won't go into screaming hysterics and throw myself off the balcony. I can handle the truth."

Alex buried his hand in her tumble of curls and sighed as he stared down into her sweet, sincere face. Had he decided that this weekend was a mistake? That he didn't want to see her anymore?

No, and that was the problem. He was in love with her. Madly, wildly, irrevocably in love with her. If she wanted the moon, he'd try to get it for her. He'd give her anything she asked for that was within his means, except for the one thing that he knew she'd want the most. Alex knew in his heart that he could never marry her.

He sighed again as he leaned his head back against the chair and returned his gaze to the ocean. He had to tell her, his conscience insisted. She had to know where she stood and make the choice of how she wanted to deal with it. If she decided to walk away from him, it would kill him, but at least he wouldn't be leading her on—letting her build herself up with false hopes for a future that would never be.

"Were you in love with Mark when you married him?" he asked.

Erica blinked, startled by the question. Was that what this was all about? Was he experiencing another bout of jealousy over Mark? As ridiculous as it sounded, it was the only conclusion that made any sense.

"Yes, I was in love with him," she answered.

"How did you feel when you realized that love had died?" he asked next.

"Hurt, sad, angry and confused."

He nodded in understanding. "I felt the same way when my marriage ended, and I suddenly understood the dark shadows I'd always seen in my mother's eyes. She was very much in love with my father, and when he betrayed that love, she never recovered from it. I almost didn't recover from Kristen, Erica, and when I did, I made a vow that I'd never make myself that vulnerable again."

He paused for a moment before continuing. "Despite my better judgment, I've fallen in love with you. But love is too fragile to trust it to last, and it hurts too badly when it turns on you. I'd like to continue to see you and Josh, but I'll never marry you or any woman, Erica, and I'll understand if you say it isn't enough for you."

His words hurt—deeply and painfully—but not for the reasons Erica would have thought they would. She, too, was wary of marriage, and though her experience hadn't turned her off to the institution as completely as Alex's evidently had, she hadn't been eager to leap back into it, either. She truly did understand his vow of confirmed bachelorhood. However, what hurt was that he honestly believed the love growing between them could never last—that it was destined to fall before it ever had a chance to really begin.

For a moment, she considered arguing with him, but then she realized that she should deal with him in the same manner that she dealt with any other problem. Don't react but act, and do it after careful deliberation.

As she continued to lie in his arms, she sorted through the pieces of his life that he'd shared with her. His mother's family had spurned him because of his very existence. His father had refused to acknowledge him. His mother had struggled to raise him while suffering from unrequited love. Then, to add fuel to the fire, his ex-wife had not only told him that she didn't want to bear his children but she'd stolen his ideas from him, and Erica knew firsthand that creativity came from your very essence. He had to have felt as if the woman had taken away a piece of his soul.

When she linked all the facts together, she realized that their relationship had been doomed from the beginning. Up until a few years ago she would have accepted that fact as a fait accompli, called it quits and moved on. But up until a few years ago she hadn't had Josh in her life. Because of him, she'd learned to overcome her insecurities and fears—to fight for what she wanted, and she wanted Alex. She couldn't guarantee that what they had would last forever, because she knew that even when you did everything right, sometimes it still went wrong. What she could guarantee, however, was that she'd fight with every fiber of her being to try to make it last forever.

But how could she make him see that without forcing him into erecting an insurmountable wall of resistance? Words wouldn't convince him, and if she responded too complacently to his vow of bachelorhood, it would be the same as saying she didn't love him enough to care.

What she had to do, she realized, was hit him at an unexpected gut level that would begin to make him question the veracity of his own words, and she had to do it in the next few seconds if she was going to maintain her edge.

For the first time in her life, she gave thanks to her mother for making her endure five interminable years of acting lessons. She might not have turned out to be another Shirley Temple, but she had developed enough skill to pull the wool over Alex's eyes.

"Oh, Alex," she gushed as she sat up on his lap and gave him a brilliant smile. "You don't know how relieved I am. I'm in love with you, too, and I'm anxious for our relationship to continue. But I have to admit that I was a bit worried you might have something more permanent in mind, and marriage just isn't on my list of life's goals."

Alex eyed her skeptically. "It isn't?"

"Of course not."

"But what about Josh?"

"What about him?"

"He needs a father, Erica."

"He has a father, even if Mark doesn't act like one. Besides, you've alleviated any doubts I had about my ability to raise Josh to upstanding manhood without a father's touch."

"How did I do that?"

"Well, just look at you. Your mother raised you without a man around the house, and you've turned out just fine. And I'm sure that if I ever run in to one of those boy problems with Josh that I'm not quite sure how to handle, you'll give me advice from a man's point of view."

"Well, of course, but . . ."

"Good. I'm glad we got this settled." She jumped off his lap, grabbed his hand and said, "You promised me another cheese omelet this morning, and I'm holding you to it. Let's get on the ball around here."

"But, Erica . . ."

"Alex, I'm starving! We can talk later."

Alex let her lead him into the apartment, even though he would have preferred staying outside and talking until they had this issue settled. What did she mean she didn't want marriage? Of course she wanted marriage. Hadn't she told him so a half-dozen times? That's why he'd been so determined to stay away from her in the first place, for Pete's sake.

But when Alex began to review their past conversations, he realized that not once had Erica used the ominous *M* word. She'd talked about commitment and family, and he'd assumed that she'd been speaking in traditional terms. But if she didn't want to get married, what did she want?

He waited until they were eating to broach the subject again. "Erica, I've been thinking about what you said on the balcony, and if you don't want to get married, what do you want? For us to live together?"

She glanced up from her plate and laughed heartily. "Are you kidding me? Why would I want to live with you?"

His temper began to stir at her laughter and lighthearted question. What did she mean, why would she want to live with him? As far as he was concerned, the answer was obvious. "Well, we do love each other, and . . ."

"And if we want to keep loving each other, we'll maintain the status quo," she interrupted cheerfully. "Please pass the salt."

"What would be so wrong about living together?" he asked, becoming more irked by the minute.

"The salt, Alex?" When he grabbed the salt shaker and practically threw it at her, she said sweetly, "Thank you. Now, as far as living together, it's a total bust as far as I can see. First, there's Josh to consider, and I'm still old-fashioned enough to believe that young children need to be instilled with a good foundation of moral values. It would be difficult for me to try to convince Josh that he shouldn't be sleeping around at the age of sixteen when I've been living in sin most of his life.

"There's also the complication of just everyday living," she continued after taking a bite of her omelet. "This is an excellent omelet, by the way. You'll have to give me your recipe."

"Yeah," Alex muttered. "What complications of everyday living are you talking about?"

"All of it," she said, spreading her arms out in an encompassing gesture. "I'd still have to do your laundry. You'd still have to take out the garbage. Then, of course, we'd have to worry about bills and budgets and if we could afford to go out to dinner or to a movie. This way, we won't even have to argue about what kind of furniture should go in the bedroom. I can keep my canopy and lace, and you can keep your four-poster and fake furs. Just think about it, Alex. If we do nothing more than continue to date, we won't have all those complications, so the courtship will never end. Makes perfect sense, doesn't it?"

It should make perfect sense, Alex realized. So why didn't it? "Then there would be no restrictions on this, uh, relationship?"

"There would be one," Erica said, suddenly sober. "I would demand total fidelity. I do have a son to raise, and I have to think of my health. I'd like to continue to see you, but I'll never compromise on fidelity with you or any other man, Alex, and I'll understand if you say it isn't enough for you."

Alex felt as if he'd just been hit with a bucket of cold water when she threw his words right back at him. Had he sounded that callous? He couldn't have, or she wouldn't be sitting here looking so chipper and totally amenable to a relationship that was based on... Just what would it be based on? he suddenly wondered.

Before he could respond, however, she wiped her napkin across her lips and said, "I really do hate to eat and run, but the truth is, I miss Josh. We've never been separated this long before. But don't worry, Alex, it'll get easier and easier as time passes. Just think, you and I have years and years of these romantic interludes to look forward to. Now, where did you put my dress?"

In the trash where it belongs, he wanted to grumble. But he'd just tacitly agreed to a relationship with her that didn't give him that right, and he didn't like it. He didn't like it at all.

"It's in the hall closet."

She rounded the table and gave him a peck on the cheek. "Great. Don't forget the recipe. I can't wait to serve it to Laura and her family the next time Josh and I have them over for Sunday brunch."

As she walked away, humming some nonsensical nursery rhyme tune, Alex realized that Erica's talk about Sunday brunch with her next-door neighbor and family hadn't included him.

"SO, HOW'S THE CRUSADE for marriage going?" Laura asked as she strolled into Erica's kitchen and dumped a plate of chocolate-chip cookies into the cookie jar.

"Thanks for the cookies," Erica answered. "Josh has

been complaining that I'm running low, but I just haven't had time to do anything about it. As far as the crusade . . . Well, I'm still hopeful. Alex has even hinted a time or two that *we*—and please note that I've used the plural—should really have you and your family over for brunch to show you *our* appreciation for all your help with Josh. He's even offered to cook his famous cheese omelet, the recipe to which he's still forgetting to write down for me."

Laura chuckled as she leaned against the counter and watched Erica stir her spaghetti sauce. "He really is a good man, Erica. I hope you can show him the error of his ways."

"Oh, Laura, so do I," Erica responded fervently as she turned to face her friend. "I love him so much, and Josh does, too. Alex is so good for both of us. Do you know that he's actually eliminated 'But I don't want to' from Josh's conversations?"

"And what has he eliminated from your life?" Laura asked.

"Everything bad. Except Mark, of course," she amended with chagrin. "The custody hearing is in two weeks, and I haven't heard a peep out of him. It isn't like him to just sit back and wait, and I keep expecting the ax to fall at any moment."

"Does your lawyer feel your chances are good?"

Erica nodded. "Actually, he thinks they're very good. Supposedly, the judge will take into consideration how traumatic it would be for Josh to not only be taken away from me, but be relocated across the country so that he wouldn't be able to see me on a regular basis. Also, Mark's failure to exercise his visitation rights is in my favor. Five visits in two years doesn't support his claim of being a loving father who will desperately miss his son.

My lawyer feels that Mark doesn't have a chance of winning."

"Oh, Erica, that's absolutely wonderful," Laura said as she stepped forward and gave Erica a hug.

"I know. I'm also happy to announce that Mother and I have agreed to disagree, but when it comes to Josh, I have the final say."

"So everything really is coming up roses."

"I have a thorn or two messing things up, but nothing I can't handle. Now, if I can just convince Alex that love is really worth taking a chance on, I'll have it made."

"I hate to play devil's advocate, but what if you can't? Are you going to take two steps backward?"

"No," Erica stated firmly. "I am strong, Laura, and my relationship with Alex has proved that. If he came to me tomorrow and said it was over, it would hurt, but I wouldn't lose it."

Laura blinked rapidly, as if fighting against tears. "Right now, I feel as proud of you as I would of one of my own kids. You've come a long way since I first met you. A very long way."

"I know," Erica replied, smiling widely. "I finally feel as if I'm all grown-up."

"WHAT'S THAT ONE look like?" Josh asked as he pointed at a billowing cloud overhead.

"An elephant," Alex said. They'd been lying on the grass and playing the game for fifteen minutes. Alex hoped he could keep Josh interested in it for another good fifteen minutes or so. During the past two hours they'd played catch, chase and hide-and-seek, and Alex was beat. He wondered how Erica kept up with the kid hour after hour, day after day, without collapsing from exhaustion.

"Nooo!" Josh said with a giggle as he rolled onto his stomach and stuck his small face in front of Alex's. "It looks like a monkey."

"A monkey?" Alex repeated in mock-disbelief. "No, it's definitely an elephant. It's too fat for a monkey. Unless it's a gorilla. I suppose it could be a gorilla."

"No, it's an elephant," Josh announced. "It's too fat for a monkey."

Alex laughed and hauled the boy onto his chest. "You are the most contrary imp I've ever met. If I say it's black, you say it's white. Your mother would say you're going through a stage, but do you know what I think it is?"

Josh shook his head.

"I think," Alex said, tapping his finger against the boy's nose, "it's a simple matter of precocity."

"What's that?" Josh asked.

"That's a bright little boy who knows more than he should, to include how to drive grown-ups crazy."

Josh giggled and sat up, straddling Alex's waist. He began to count the buttons on the front of Alex's shirt, and Alex watched him, a fond smile curving his lips.

When Erica had asked him to baby-sit while she met with her attorney, he'd eagerly agreed. He enjoyed these times with Josh. Everything in the child's life was so basic. If he was hurt, he cried. If he was happy, he laughed. He could get into trouble quicker than a cage full of monkeys, but he was usually motivated by plain old curiosity. The world was like a big toy store to him, and he wanted to experience it all.

It was amazing to Alex, but Josh had also begun to change the way that he, Alex, looked at life. Josh didn't know that there were shades of gray. He saw everything simply and, more often than not, went right to the crux of the matter. More and more frequently, Alex had found himself doing the same thing, both in business and in his personal life. And he acknowledged with chagrin, his personal life—or to be more specific, Erica—was definitely muddled.

He loved her, and he had no doubt that she loved him. All he had to do was watch the way her face lit up the instant she saw him after they'd been apart to know that simple truth. The trouble was, he was beginning to resent their times apart, but whenever he'd suggest that they spend more time together, she always had a hundred excuses why they couldn't. She had deadlines to meet, laundry or grocery shopping to do, bills to pay, correspondence to catch up on, and the list went on and on and on. Then she'd try to pacify him by saying that as soon as the child-custody hearing was over, she'd arrange to spend another romantic weekend with him.

Alex had come to the conclusion that he'd trade a year's worth of romantic weekends with her just to have her by his side day after day. To wake up with her in the morning and go to sleep with her at night. To know that all he had to do was reach out and she'd be there.

But in order to do that, he'd have to marry her, and he still hadn't been able to convince himself that marriage was the answer. And even if he did, how would he convince Erica that it was? She had, after all, made it quite clear that she wasn't interested in a trip to the altar, which he found the most frustrating of all.

"What do you say about going inside and having some milk and cookies?" Alex asked Josh, experiencing a sudden need to move—to work off some of the frustration of his troubling thoughts.

"Three cookies," Josh announced, holding up the appropriate number of fingers.

"*Two* cookies," Alex corrected, holding up his own fingers. "It's too close to dinnertime, and your mother will shoot me if I spoil your appetite."

When Josh looked disappointed, Alex relented with, "Well, I suppose you and I could split a third cookie. Okay?"

"Okay," Josh answered with a bright laugh as he scrambled off Alex and ran toward the door. "Catch me!"

As Alex leaped to his feet and took off after the toddler, he found himself wishing that the boy's mother would offer the same challenge. That way he wouldn't have to make any decisions. He could simply react.

ERICA COULDN'T BREATHE. She kept telling her brain that it was a simple function. You inhaled, and then you exhaled, but it refused to acknowledge the instructions.

She'd known that Mark's silence had been too good to be true, but she hadn't suspected that he'd turn on her like this—that he'd use the very means that she'd chosen to get the money to fight him against her.

"Erica, are you okay?" her attorney, Daniel Adams, asked in concern.

Erica managed to nod, even though she knew it was an absolute lie. Mark was going to win. He was going to take Josh away from her and she'd probably never see him again. How in the world could she survive without Josh? How?

"Mark's going to win, isn't he?" she said miserably. "He's going to take those child psychologists' statements into court and he's going to walk out with Josh."

"I have to admit that it doesn't look good," Daniel replied.

"What can I do? There has to be something I can do," she stated frantically as she leaned toward his desk.

"There has to be a way I can fight back. The My Fair Baby commercials haven't hurt Josh. He's loved doing them. If he didn't, I would have never let him do them. They haven't hurt him in any way!"

"That may be true, Erica, but you aren't a trained professional qualified to make that judgment. Your ex-husband has gotten opinions from two top child psychologists in the country, and they both state that forcing Josh to do those commercials could cause him irreparable damage. Mr. Stewart also has a point when he states that you, of all people, should be aware of that."

"This is a nightmare," Erica muttered as she rose to her feet and began to pace. "An absolute nightmare. The only reason I let Josh do the commercials in the first place was because I needed the money to fight Mark. And I didn't force Josh to do them," she stated adamantly. "He *wanted* to do them."

Daniel let out a sigh and said, "Children also want to play in the street, Erica, but we don't let them do so, because we know they can get hurt."

Erica came to a dead halt and stared at him in disbelief. "You agree with Mark, don't you?"

"No," Daniel replied. "I'm merely giving you a taste of how your ex-husband's attorney will counter your claim. The way I see it, your only option is to take Josh out of the commercials and tell the judge that the moment you heard what these child psychologists had to say, you took immediate action because you would never purposely do anything to endanger Josh's mental health. However, you may have difficulty breaking your contract with the advertising agency, and if they decide to sue, you'll just be handing your ex-husband even more ammunition."

"Breaking the contract won't be a problem," Erica responded, secure enough in Alex's love for both her and Josh to know that he'd release her from the contract. But at what expense to himself? Josh had just started on the last commercial, and it should be done before the hearing. Now, at the last minute, Alex was going to have to go to My Fair Baby and tell them that he couldn't deliver it. If they refused to understand the situation he could lose everything, including his business which, Erica knew, meant she would lose him. Alex was too proud a man to take on a family when he didn't have the means to support them, and even if she could overcome that barrier, would he ever be able to forgive her for destroying all his hopes and dreams?

12

"I REALLY APPRECIATE you taking Josh for the night, Laura," Alex said as she stood in the doorway of Josh's bedroom while he packed an overnight bag for the boy. "I know Erica wouldn't have asked you to do so if it wasn't important."

"Alex, I told you that I'm happy to keep Josh," Laura said. "Erica is not only one of my best friends, she's like a kid sister to me. She didn't give you any hint about what her attorney said?"

Alex shook his head. "All she said was that we needed to talk, and she asked me to call you and see if you'd keep Josh for the night."

"How did she sound?"

"Calm," Alex answered grimly. "Too calm. If I could get my hands on Mark Stewart right now, I'd wring his neck. If he loved his son half as much as Erica does, he'd know that Josh belongs here with her. Why is he putting her through this?"

"Erica says it's revenge," Laura replied. "Personally, I think that in his own warped way, Mark is still in love with her. Why else would he have waited two years to pull this stunt?"

Alex sat on Josh's bed and stared at the woman in stunned surprise. "You think he still loves her? Why?"

"What's not to love?" Laura asked with a shrug. "And it had to be love to make an inveterate playboy like Mark marry her in the first place. I've suspected all along that Mark is using the custody suit to try to get Erica back."

"But he's supposedly engaged to be married," Alex pointed out.

"Supposedly is the key word, Alex. Engagements can be broken. Put yourself in Mark's shoes," Laura suggested. "He's still in love with Erica, but she's walked out on him and has managed to move on with her life. She's grown stronger by the day, so he can no longer get her to bend to his will. The only muscle he has left to flex is Josh. What better way to not only get Erica back, but ensure that she'll stay, than to win legal control over what she holds most dear in her heart? And if you were Erica, what would you do?"

"Go back to him," Alex answered absently, as his mind reeled with the repercussions. "She'd go back to him in a flash and wouldn't even think twice about it."

"Exactly," Laura agreed. "Erica doesn't love Mark any longer, but she lives for Josh. She'd go to hell and back for him. I just pray that she doesn't have to make that choice, because she deserves more than that."

"Yes," Alex murmured softly. "She deserves a lot more than that." She deserves a hell of a lot more than that, he reiterated once Laura and Josh had left.

ERICA DIDN'T LOOK FORWARD to her talk with Alex. In fact, she'd rather be doing anything than dropping this bombshell on him. It was bad enough that Mark was wreaking havoc on her life, but it was unforgivable that his actions were going to interfere with Alex's life.

She should have never agreed to the commercials in the first place, she told herself as she turned on to her street. She should have stuck with her original decision not to let Josh have any part of them. She should have...

But should haves weren't going to change anything, she reminded herself. She'd made her choices and they'd backfired on her. She could only pray that they weren't going to destroy everything good that she'd found with Alex. That even if the worst did happen and he lost everything, he'd be able to forgive her, because she would never be able to live with the fact that he hated her.

When she pulled into her driveway, she expected Alex to come flying out the front door. Thankfully, he didn't, giving her a chance to draw on the remainder of her courage. She assured herself that he'd release her from the contract, because he cared about Josh as much as she did. He'd give her every chance possible to make sure that Mark didn't take him away from her. She drew in a deep breath to bolster her confidence, climbed out of the car and headed for the house.

Alex heard Erica's car, but he didn't move from his seat on the sofa. His mind was in such an uproar that he didn't trust himself to greet her. Laura's words had been taunting him ever since she'd left. *And if you were Erica what would you do?*

She was going to go back to Mark. Alex knew it. He was convinced of it. He'd lay odds on it. Big odds. Mark Stewart was going to win, and not only was he going to get Josh, but he was going to get Erica, even though she didn't love him. Even though she didn't belong with him.

And what was Alex going to have when it was over? Only his business, but it was his and no one could take it away from him. He'd pour his life and soul into it. He'd make Harte Advertising the biggest name in the advertising world. It had to work out that way, because if it didn't, what else would he have?

Nothing.

When she walked in the door, all he had to do was take one look at her face to know he was right. It was over. Why had he let himself get involved with her in the first place? Why had he let himself fall in love?

But all the whys in the world weren't going to change anything. He had fallen in love with her, and now she was going to make him eat his words. She was going to prove to him again how badly it hurt to have love turn on you.

"Hi," she said, leaning back against the door.

"Just give me the bad news and get it over with," Alex stated roughly, raking a hand through his hair. "I need a drink, and your house is dry, as usual."

Erica automatically bristled at the criticism. "You know I rarely keep alcohol in the house because it's one of the leading killers of children."

"Of course, and we always have to think of Josh, right?" he drawled sarcastically. "He comes first and foremost. Tell me, Erica, what are you going to do when he's grown-up and gone? Sit by the phone and wait for his calls?"

"Why are you being so mean?" she asked, her eyes reflecting her hurt.

"You tell me," Alex replied, refusing to give in to the need to comfort her. She was going to leave him, he reminded himself. She was going to choose a man she abhorred over him. Once again, he was going to be stuck in second place. "What did your attorney say?"

"That things don't look good. Mark has..."

"Mark has what?" he snapped impatiently when she didn't continue. "Dammit, Erica, I have a business to run, and I don't have the time to sit around waiting for you to play your damsel-in-distress routine. Just tell me what the man said so I can get the hell out of here."

"Damsel-in-distress routine?" she repeated angrily. "Just what do you mean by that?"

"You know exactly what I mean," he roared as he came to his feet. "Ever since I've met you I've had to coddle you and hold your hand. I've listened to all the poor little Erica stories until I'm sick of them. You had a rough life, and I'm sorry for that. But do you think you're the only person the world has kicked around? If you do, you're sorely mistaken. I've had my share of kicks, too, but I haven't crawled into a corner to lick my wounds. Maybe Mark is right. Maybe Josh does belong with him."

Erica paled. "You don't mean that. You *can't* mean that. You love Josh, Alex, and you know it."

"The kid's great," he answered. "But he isn't the greatest thing to come along since Einstein. And to tell you the truth, Erica, he can be a real pain in the neck."

Erica could handle Alex turning on her, but when he turned on Josh, he was entering into an entirely different ball game. She immediately came to the boy's defense.

"Josh can be a handful, Alex, and I'll be the first to acknowledge that. But he's basically a good kid, and you know it. If you're angry, fine. Take it out on me, but don't—and I repeat—don't denigrate him. He's just a little boy, so be a man and pick on someone your own size."

He swore softly and violently and walked to the windows. As he stared out them, he said, "You're right. I'm angry and I'm taking it out on Josh. I apologize. What did your attorney say?"

"Mark has statements from two of the top child psychologists in the country. They're saying that the commercials could cause irreparable damage to Josh." When Alex's back stiffened, she quickly said, "I know it isn't true, Alex, but I'm pushed against a wall. I either break

Josh's contract or I lose him. I want you to release us from the last commercial."

"No," Alex said as he pivoted around to face her.

"No?" Erica repeated in disbelief. "Alex, you have to let us out of the contract or I'm going to lose Josh!"

"So?" he drawled. "Your custody battle over Josh has nothing to do with me, Erica. You signed a contract, and you are going to live up to it. If you don't, I'll sue. I'm not giving up everything I worked for so you can battle it out with your ex-husband."

"But that's not fair!" she yelled at him.

"Life isn't fair," he yelled back. "Mark is playing a game with you, and if you give in to him now, you're going to be fighting him until Josh has reached the age of emancipation. If you want to be a victim, that's your choice, but I'm not going to let you drag me down with you.

"I'll hire psychologists to dispute his claims," he continued. "I'll bring them on the set where they can observe Josh firsthand. I'll pay for it out of my own pocket, Erica, but I will not cave in to Mark Stewart. The contract stands. If you walk away from it, I'll make sure that you regret it. By the time I'm through with you, you'll be wishing you were facing Mark in court instead of me."

"You don't care," she stated dully as his refusal sank in. "You don't care about us at all. We've been your pawns, and you've been moving us across the board as if we were in a chess game. Why, Alex? Is winning that important to you? Is success worth more to you than people?"

"Yes!" he answered vehemently as he crossed the room, caught her chin and raised her face to his. "Success is important to me. It always has been and it always will be. But before you condemn me for that, think about your own motivations, Erica. You've used me, too. If you hadn't been fighting Mark, you would have never agreed to the commercials. You would have sat here in your safe little world with your safe little monsters. You would have drawn your heart out, but you never would have had to feel. And you have felt with me, Erica. I've given you more than you'll ever find with anyone else."

He released her, jerking his hand away as if touching her was suddenly repulsive. "Run on out to your garage, Erica. Turn me into a monster. Make me into everything that's bad. But while you're doing it, also think about the way you've melted in my arms. Remember what it's like, so that when you're lying in Mark's arms twenty years from now, you can eat your heart out."

With that, he slammed out her front door, and Erica stared at it in confusion and anger.

What in the world was he talking about? Lying in Mark's arms twenty years from now? She'd rather rot in hell.

And that was just where she'd be rotting, she realized when the import of all his words came crashing down on her. He wouldn't release her from the contract, which meant she was stuck between the proverbial rock and a hard place. If Josh continued with the commercials, Mark would rake her over the coals. If she didn't continue with the commercials, Alex would rake her over the coals.

Tears welled into Erica's eyes and she slammed her fist against the wall. Mark and Alex were punishing her, and Josh was going to be the victim. He was going to pay the price for her sins.

What she needed was her sketchpad, but when she crossed to the coffee table and lifted it, Alex's words came back to haunt her. *Run on out to your garage, Erica. Turn me into a monster. Make me into everything that's bad.*

She dropped the sketchpad back to the coffee table as if burned. Was this what she'd finally come to? Had she reached the point that every confrontation was a monster? Had her sketchpad become as addictive to her as a bottle to an alcoholic?

Maybe Alex was right. Maybe Josh did belong with Mark.

But she didn't believe that. She loved Josh with all her heart and always would. She might not be the best mother in the world, but she deserved good grades for trying. If Josh went to live with Mark, he'd be raised by nannies, and then moved on to boarding school.

What she needed was someone to talk to, and she dialed the number by rote. When her mother came on the line, she burst into tears as she sobbed, "Mama, I need to talk to you. I don't know what to do."

ALEX BELLOWED for his secretary. When she stuck her head in the door, he said, "Pamela, I told you over an hour ago that I needed the Miller Electronics proposal."

"It's on your desk. Right under your nose, as a matter of fact. While I'm here, is there anything else you'd like to scream for?"

Alex had the good grace to blush. "Sorry. I guess I'm in a bad mood."

"Try unlivable mood," Pamela stated dryly. "Try unlivable for the past two weeks. One of us needs a vacation, Alex, and I'm not taking mine until Christmas."

"Has anyone ever told you that you're a pain in the..."

"My husband has," she interrupted coolly, "and it's usually when he's behaving just like you. I don't know what your problem is, Alex, but I'll tell you exactly what

I tell him. Whatever it is, handle it. I don't get paid to be a whipping boy."

She slammed the door shut and Alex leaned back in his chair with a sigh. He knew he was behaving like a kid in the throes of a temper tantrum, but the past two weeks had been hell. Since his argument with Erica, he hadn't gone near the studio. According to Ron they needed at least two more shoots to wind up the commercial, and Erica's custody hearing was tomorrow. If the judge ruled against her, both their worlds would come crashing down around their ears. He knew, however, that his world could be patched together much more easily than hers.

He reached for his copy of the reports from the three child psychologists he'd hired to evaluate Josh's work on the commercials. All were glowing reports on the method in which the commercials were handled, as well as supportive as to Josh's mental well-being.

He couldn't help but grin when he read the line where one of them had stated, "Joshua Stewart is an active, precocious child who, by the very nature of his intelligence, is fast developing skills in manipulation to repudiate any knowledge of misbehavior. To put this in layman's terms, the kid is spoiled rotten and knows it, but he is not unruly or unmanageable. In fact, I wish my own son was as easy to handle, and I commend Ms Stewart on her parenting skills."

Yes, Josh was spoiled rotten, Alex agreed. But it wasn't the kind of spoiled that turned a person off. It was the kind of spoiled that made a person laugh and want to hug him to their chest. He was full of vim and vinegar, but just when you wanted to shake him by his ears, he tossed his arms around your neck and told you how much he loved you.

And today might be the last day he'd be on the set. It might be the very last time Alex would have the chance to see him. Pamela had told him to handle the problem, and Alex knew that it was time he did exactly that.

"MADELAINE, WHERE'S ERICA?" Alex asked in surprise when he came on the set and found Josh's grandmother instead of his mother.

"Home," Madelaine answered as she stared at him accusingly. "The custody hearing is tomorrow, but as you can see, Erica is doing everything she can to uphold her contract."

"I know that," Alex answered, stuffing his hands into his pockets. He refused to feel guilty. He'd done for himself what he had to do to survive. He felt sorry for Erica and her circumstances, but they really didn't have anything to do with him. And if the truth be told, the only one at fault around here was Madelaine. If she hadn't auditioned Josh without his mother's permission, none of them would be in this mess.

When Madelaine turned her attention back to the set, Alex asked, "How's Erica holding up?"

"She's not," Madelaine answered simply. "She looks like death warmed over, and she hasn't been able to eat for two weeks. Anything she puts in her mouth comes right back up. The doctor says it's nerves. She has had it checked out. She's not stupid, you know."

"Madelaine, there are a lot of words I'd use to describe Erica, but stupid isn't one of them."

"And how would you describe yourself?" Madelaine asked. Before he could answer, she said, "Josh is staying with me tonight. Erica's too upset, and she's afraid that her attitude will transfer to him. She doesn't want it to affect his appearance in court. Did you know that he has to appear in court?"

Alex's gaze automatically shifted to Josh and Kitty, who were involved in a complicated game of dress-up to promote My Fair Baby's children's formal attire. "No, I didn't know that Josh would have to appear in court, but I suppose it makes sense. After all, the hearing is about him."

"Well, according to Erica's attorney, his appearance could be the deciding factor. If you don't mind, Alex, I'd like to concentrate on the shoot. I'll be happy to talk to you later."

"Yeah. Later," Alex said as he turned and headed out of the building to his car.

When he climbed in, he told himself to go right to the office. His car, however, seemed to have a mind of its own and took the most direct route to Erica's house. He walked hesitantly up the path and rang the bell. She didn't answer, and he'd just decided to leave when the door opened.

"What do you want?" Erica asked, bravely sniffing against tears.

Her mother was right, he decided. She looked like death warmed over. What kind of an appearance was this to make in court? The judge would take one look at her and hand Josh over to Mark—lock, stock and toy box.

"I thought you might need a friend," he answered.

Erica told herself to turn him away. She told herself that she was facing the blackest day of her life because of him. She told herself how she didn't love him, and reminded herself of how he'd not only used her but her son.

But no matter how many reasons she gave herself to slam the door in his face, when he turned to walk away, she automatically reached for him. "Alex, please. I . . ."

The moment she touched him, Alex was lost, and he spun around and caught her up into his arms as she burst into tears.

"Shh," he whispered against her hair. "It's going to be all right, Erica. I promise, it's going to be all right. No matter what happens tomorrow, you aren't going to lose Josh."

"Promise me," she begged as she clutched at his lapels. "Please, Alex, promise me."

"I promise," he said, knowing that only he understood that when Mark won, he'd be winning back both his son and his wife. He swung her up into his arms and carried her to her bedroom. "You need some rest, Erica. You can't go into court looking like a woman who's lost her wits."

"But I can't close my eyes," she said pitifully. "Every time I do, I hear Josh calling for me and he's lost. I can't find him, Alex. I keep looking for him, but I can't find him."

"It's just a dream," he assured as he tucked her beneath the covers, clothes and all. He sat down beside her and brushed her hair away from her ravaged face. "It's just a dream, and I'll wake you up if you have it again. Get some sleep, Erica. You need some sleep."

"Will you come to court with me tomorrow?" she asked, her eyes drifting closed as he continued to stroke her hair. "Please, Alex, just come with me tomorrow, and I promise I'll never ask you to do anything for me ever again."

No! Alex's mind screamed. He'd had his own nightmares recently, and one of them had been watching Mark walk out of the courtroom holding Josh on one arm and Erica on the other. They walked right past him and out into the sunshine as a family.

"I'll come with you," he replied.

"Thank you," she whispered, and for the first time in two weeks, she was able to fall fast asleep.

"ALEX!" JOSH SCREAMED when Alex and Erica entered the courthouse.

The boy broke away from his grandmother and raced toward them. Alex automatically caught him and lifted him up into his arms. "Hi, there, sport."

Josh threw his arms around Alex's neck and nearly choked him with an exuberant hug as he declared, "I missed you."

"I missed you, too," Alex stated gruffly as he gave the boy an exuberant hug of his own. "Have you been a good boy?"

Josh looked him right in the eye, giggled and said, "No."

Alex chuckled and hugged him again. "You're a holy terror, but at least you're an honest one, right?"

"Uh-huh," Josh answered.

Erica watched the exchange, with tears in her eyes. This was the way things should be, and she wished for a fairy godmother to pop up, wave her magic wand and whisk the three of them away. To take them back to the time when they were all happy together. Before all the angry words had been spoken and the bitter wall had risen between her and Alex.

And she knew that wall was still there, despite his presence here today. He'd been too quiet around her—too stoic. Not once had he reached for her or tried to kiss her, and the one time she'd reached out and touched him, he'd leaped away from her as if she'd given him an electrical shock. She wasn't sure what his reasons were for agreeing to come with her, but she was sure that it wasn't out of love, and it broke her heart.

Her attorney joined them and said, "It's time for us to go inside, Erica."

Panic rushed through her, and she automatically glanced toward Alex. He gave her an encouraging smile and a thumb's up sign. It didn't make the panic go away, but it did help her gain control over it.

"I love you," she told Josh as she gave him a kiss and a hug. "You stay out here with Grandma and Alex, and you behave, understand?"

Josh nodded and rested his head on Alex's shoulder.

"Good luck," Alex told her softly.

"Yeah. I'm going to need it."

ALEX WANTED TO PACE as he watched the big hand on the old clock hanging on the wall quiver and drop down another minute, but Josh had been hanging on to him since he'd walked into the courthouse and refused to let Alex put him down. Right now the boy was entertaining himself by pushing the knot in Alex's tie back and forth on his neck.

"How much longer do you think this is going to take?" he asked Madelaine, who'd been sitting beside him in silence. Usually, she talked a mile a minute, and Alex was a bit unnerved by the fact that she wasn't doing so now. "They've been in there for over an hour."

Madelaine shrugged. "If Mark is going to win, I hope it never ends, and if he does win, it's going to be my fault. If I'd been a better mother, Erica wouldn't have fallen for the first man who came along and showed her any kindness. If I'd . . ."

Alex reached out and squeezed her hand. "Don't do that to yourself, Madelaine. We all make mistakes. We wouldn't be human if we didn't."

"Human!" Josh repeated with a delighted laugh as he gave a sudden jerk on Alex's tie, nearly strangling him as the knot lodged against his Adam's apple.

Alex had just managed to loosen the knot and was gasping for breath when the door to the judge's chamber opened and a uniformed woman stepped out, saying, "We're ready for Joshua."

But when she tried to take him, Josh yelled, "No! I want Alex!" and threw his arms around Alex's neck, hanging on for dear life.

"Josh, you have to go with the woman," Alex insisted as he struggled to release Josh's hold on him. He'd have a better chance of getting away from an octopus, he decided, when his efforts only made Josh hang on more tightly and Alex was once again being strangled.

"No," Josh stated stubbornly.

"But, Josh, your mama's in there." Madelaine said as she tried to help pry the toddler loose. She wasn't having any more success than Alex. "Don't you want to go see your mama?"

"No!" he screamed at the top of his lungs. "I want Alex!"

"What's the problem?" an unfamiliar voice asked, and Alex glanced up to see a gray-haired, middle-aged woman standing in front of him clad in a judge's robe.

Great! he thought irritably. This is just great! Erica's spent the past hour trying to prove what a good mother she is, and now Josh is going to throw a temper tantrum and blow her right out of the water.

"I think he's nervous," Alex said, still trying to release Josh's hold on him. He managed to get one arm loose, but while he tried to pull the other one free, Josh wrapped his legs around Alex's middle with enough force to make him wince.

The judge chuckled. "It appears that the only way we'll get Josh into my chambers is if you come with him. Why don't you just bring him in, Mr. . . ."

"Harte," he supplied as he rose to his feet. "Alexander Harte. I'm sorry about this, Your Honor, but he's in a possessive stage, and right now I'm what he's decided to possess. He's not normally this unruly."

The judge arched a brow. "Well, let's get him into my chambers so I can have a talk with him."

Alex followed her, his stomach clenching nervously over this unexpected event. When he walked in and Erica gaped at him in shock, he gave a helpless shrug.

The judge sat down behind her desk and said, "It seems Joshua has decided that where he goes, Mr. Harte goes, so I've asked Mr. Harte to join us. I'm sure none of you will have any objections. After all, we don't want to upset Joshua any more than we have to, do we?"

Alex was pleased to note that Mark's attorney, who'd started to rise to his feet as if to object, quickly sat down. Alex cast a covert look at Erica's attorney, and the man winked at him. Somehow that made Alex relax, and he took the chair next to the judge's desk when she gestured him toward it.

Josh, evidently satisfied that he'd gotten his way, released his hold on Alex and settled down on his lap. He looked at the judge and asked, "Who're you?"

"I'm Judge Gilliam, but you can call me Mary. Do you know why you're here today, Josh?"

"No," he replied. "What's that?" he asked as he leaned toward the judge's desk and touched her gavel.

"It's called a gavel, and it's like a hammer."

"Ouch," Josh said as he jerked his hand away from it. "Hammers hurt."

"Have you ever hurt yourself with a hammer?" the judge asked.

"No," Josh answered.

"Then how do you know they hurt?"

"Mama told me. Huh, Mama?" he said as he glanced toward her with a wide grin.

"That's right," Erica murmured, catching her bottom lip between her teeth when it trembled. She wasn't going to cry, she told herself. When the judge had left the room to get Josh, Daniel had said he felt they had a good chance of winning if Josh's interview went well. He might get upset if she started to cry, and she couldn't afford to have him upset.

He suddenly scrambled off Alex's lap and ran over to the California state flag that stood beside the judge's desk. "It's *sooo* pretty," he said as he reached out and touched it.

The judge leaned back in her chair and studied him. "Yes, it is pretty," she finally said. "I hear you've been making commercials, Josh. Is that true?"

"Yeah," he said grinning at her. "Me and Kitty are going to be on TV. Huh, Mama?"

"Yes," Erica answered.

"Did you have fun making the commercials?" the judge asked next.

"Yeah." He sat on the floor and untied his shoelaces. "I can tie my shoes. Want to see?"

The judge chuckled. "Sure."

Josh chewed on his bottom lip as he concentrated on tying his laces. They weren't perfect bows, Erica noted, but at least he had the concept mastered.

When he was done, the judge said, "That's very good, Josh. Now, I'd like you to do a favor for me. I want you to look around the room, and when you see your daddy, I want you to go to him, okay?"

Josh frowned at her. "Why?"

"Because it's a game," the judge answered. "You like to play games, don't you?"

Josh nodded.

"Good. Now, look around the room, find your daddy and run to him."

Erica caught her breath and held it as Josh glanced around the room. She and her attorney were claiming that Mark had spent so little time with Josh that his son didn't even recognize him. Mark was claiming that he'd visited so rarely because Erica made his visits too difficult, but he had assured the judge that Josh knew who he was.

"Well, Josh?" the judge prodded.

"Daddy!" Josh suddenly yelled as he made a mad dash for Alex.

"I object!" Mark yelled as he leaped to his feet.

"Well, I should hope so," the judge stated dryly.

Alex, shocked by Josh's actions, could only stare at the boy in disbelief when he scrambled back into his lap and gave him a big kiss. Then Josh sat down on Alex's lap and beamed at the judge.

Mark walked to them, a muscle jumping angrily in his jaw, but his voice was pure honey when he said, "That was really cute, Josh, but I'm your daddy." He held out his arms. "Come here and give me a hug."

Josh shook his head against Alex's chest. "No. I don't like you. You're not nice."

Mark laughed nervously and bent his knees so that he was at Josh's eye level. He reached out to touch Josh, but the boy slapped his hand away. "No. Go away."

"Josh, now is not the time to play games," Mark said, his voice tinged with impatience. "Now please, be a good boy and come here."

Josh shook his head again.

"I think you should return to your seat, Mr. Stewart," the judge said.

Mark swiveled his head toward her and opened his mouth as if to object, but then snapped it closed and did as she'd suggested.

The judge turned her attention on Alex, and Alex had to fight against the urge to squirm in his chair beneath her cool, assessing gaze.

"What is your relationship with the Stewart family, Mr. Harte?" she asked.

Alex gulped. How was he supposed to answer that? I'm Erica's ex-lover? He switched his attention to Erica, who was sitting stiff and pale in her chair, her chin tilted proudly as though she were preparing to walk to the guillotine, and with good reason if he told the truth. But he was talking to a judge, and wasn't he obligated to tell the truth, the whole truth and nothing but the truth?

Yes. But what, exactly, was the truth?

He glanced down at Josh, who was resting contentedly against him and humming an off-key version of some song that Alex recognized as coming from *The Wizard of Oz*. He also recalled when he had rented the videotape and the three of them had sat in front of the television eating popcorn and watching it.

The truth was, the happiest days of Alex's life had been those he'd shared with Erica and Josh. He loved them both with all his heart, and he was never going to stop loving them. He wanted to marry Erica. He wanted to make the three of them a family, and he was going to do so if he had to drag Erica to the altar kicking and screaming.

"I'm engaged to Erica," he announced.

Erica gasped in disbelief, but when she parted her lips to speak, Alex sent her a quelling look. What in the world was the man trying to do? she asked herself in frustration. Ruin everything?

"Congratulations on your upcoming nuptials," the judge said. She straightened in her chair and announced, "I'm going to take a few minutes to deliberate this case, so I'd appreciate it if you'd all step out into the hallway. I'll summon you as soon as I've made my decision."

Josh crawled off Alex's lap and ran to his mother as she stood. Alex scrutinized both of them, but he was more concerned with Erica. There was high color in her cheeks and she was refusing to look in his direction.

Alex shrugged, rose to his feet and walked into the hallway. He leaned against the wall and waited as the remaining people filed out. Mark and his attorney were the first to leave, and the glare Mark tossed at Alex was deadly enough to kill. Alex smiled at the man.

When Erica and her attorney came out, she still refused to look at him, but Alex found that he didn't mind. After all, the woman had told him that she didn't want to get married, and it wasn't going to be the easiest chore in the world to make her see the light.

But he *was* going to marry her, even if the judge ruled in Mark's favor and she lost Josh. They'd file a new custody suit. And if Mark won that round, they'd file another and keep filing them until they had Josh back. Erica belonged to him, and he wasn't going to let her sacrifice her life to a man who didn't deserve her.

Erica couldn't decide what had her more jumpy—the wait for the judge to finally resolve Josh's custody or Alex, whose eyes she could feel boring into her back. Why had he pulled that stunt in there? What had he hoped to gain from it?

The only answer she could come up with was the My Fair Baby commercials. Ron had told her that they didn't have enough good film to splice together both a thirty-second and a sixty-second spot of the last commercial. If she won custody of Josh, then the commercials would be completed. If she lost, then they wouldn't. Alex had been trying to cover his own bases, she realized, and suddenly she was furious with him.

Her attorney had informed her that Alex's engagement announcement would probably turn the tables in her favor, particularly after seeing how fond Josh was of Alex. But when time passed and they didn't get married, Mark would most likely haul her back into court and she'd have to go through all of this again.

It was time, she decided, that she tell Mr. Alexander Harte just what she thought about him and his darn commercials. And if she did win custody of Josh? Well, she'd walk out on Alex's contract. Let the man sue her!

She marched toward him, murder in her eye.

Alex grinned inwardly as he watched Erica swoop down on him. She was mad. Hopping mad. Mad enough to be a model for one of her own book covers. Good. He wanted her mad. He wanted her furious. He wanted her ready to scratch his eyes out. Mad he could handle, because if she was mad, she'd talk. She'd say exactly what was in her heart and on her mind. Hopefully she'd say enough that he'd be able to turn her words back on her.

And if she didn't? Well, he had other methods to handle her.

"I know exactly what you were doing in there," she muttered lowly when she reached him. "And I want you to know that you are the most despicable man I have ever known. It's bad enough that you've been using me and Josh from the very beginning, but I'm telling you right now, buster, that you won't be using us anymore!

"If I win custody of Josh, we're walking, Alex," she continued after pausing long enough to catch her breath. "You can take me to court, but I'll fight you tooth and nail. I'll tie you up in so much red tape that Josh will be graduating from college before you get a ruling on the My Fair Baby commercials. I'll . . ."

Alex had heard enough. He pulled her into his arms and kissed her—hard and long and with every ounce of love in his heart. Her struggle was brief, and then she was leaning against him, as malleable as hot steel against an anvil.

Somehow, Alex was able to hang onto enough sanity to remember where they were, and when she made a passionate little murmur in the back of her throat, he forced himself to pull away from the kiss.

When she looked up at him, eyes glazed, he said, "I release you from the contract, Erica. From this moment on, you have no obligation to the My Fair Baby commercials. Your only obligation is to me. I love you, and I always will. I meant what I said in there. I want to marry you, and I know you want to marry me."

"But . . ." Erica began in confusion, only to be interrupted when the judge opened the door to her chambers and asked everyone to come back in.

Alex eased her out of his embrace. "I'll be waiting here for you."

Erica looked from him to her attorney, who was gesturing for her to hurry. She glanced back up at Alex in confusion, only to have him give her a gentle push toward the door.

"The judge is waiting," he told her. "And it isn't polite to keep a judge waiting. I'll keep my fingers crossed that the woman is as smart as she looks. Good luck."

Erica didn't want to leave until he'd explained himself, but she knew that she had to handle first things first, and Josh was still her number-one priority. As she walked through the door, she glanced over her shoulder, and Alex held up crossed fingers while smiling at her.

"Well, what do you think is going to happen?" Madelaine asked as she approached him.

"I don't know," Alex answered. "But I will tell you this. Win or lose, I'm going to marry your daughter, even if I have to hog-tie her to do so."

"Well, it's about time," Madelaine said.

Josh chose that moment to tip over an ashtray filled with sand.

"Joshua Thomas Stewart, just what do you think you're doing?" Madelaine demanded.

He looked up at her and smiled angelically. "It fell down all by itself."

Alex burst into laughter and was still laughing when Mark Stewart came flying out of the judge's chamber. He stopped right in front of Alex and stabbed his finger against Alex's chest. "You haven't seen the last of me yet."

Alex arched a brow. "Well, as Josh's father, you'll always be welcome in our home. We'll look forward to your visits."

Mark's curse was vile as he stormed away and Alex watched Erica stumble out of the room with a dazed look on her face.

"Well?" Madelaine demanded when she stopped in front of them and just shook her head.

"I won," she said in amazement. "Not only is Josh mine, but until Josh feels comfortable enough to go with Mark on his own, I have to be present whenever he visits. The judge also doubled his child support, and Mark came unglued. When he objected, she tripled it, and told him that if he ever wasted the court's time again, she'd quadruple it."

"Oh, Erica, that's wonderful!" Madelaine exclaimed tearfully as she threw her arms around her daughter. "I love you so much, and it was killing me to have you go through this."

"I love you, Mama," she whispered as she hugged her back. "I love you, too."

Madelaine pushed Erica away and dashed at tears. "Well, I'm going home. If you feel like it, stop by and we'll celebrate. I've got some champagne in the refrigerator."

Erica nodded and when Madelaine left, she glanced around for Josh. He was sitting on the floor and playing with the sand from the ashtray.

"Joshua Thomas Stewart, just what have you done?" she demanded.

"It fell down all by itself," Alex said as he grabbed her arm and turned her around to face him. He touched the curls framing her face, loving the way they clung to his fingers. In fact, he loved everything about her. "Now, about our engagement . . ."

Erica drew in a deep breath and let it out slowly. "Yes, about that. Look, Alex, I know you were trying to help in there, and you did help. But I'm not going to hold you to anything. I know how you feel about marriage and..."

"What is it, Josh?" Alex asked when the boy began to tug on his pants leg.

"Catch me!" the boy yelled and took off for the door.

"Joshua, you come back here right this instant!" Erica yelled as she took off after him.

Alex chuckled and shook his head. Who would have ever thought that getting engaged was going to be so hard to do?

He joined the race, easily passing Erica and scooping Josh up into his arms a second before the boy reached the door.

"Joshua, when I get my hands on you, I'm going to turn you over my knee," Erica threatened.

Josh giggled as he wrapped his arms around Alex's neck and said, "Run, Daddy. Run. Don't let her catch me."

"Should I run, Erica?" he asked as he turned to face her, Josh held securely in his arms. "You know, if you catch him, you catch me. We come as a packaged deal."

Erica stopped in her tracks and searched his face. The love reflected on it was as pure as the love on Josh's face. Josh wasn't Alex's biological son, but in his heart, where it really mattered, she knew that he considered Josh his.

"Are you sure you're ready for this?" she asked, determined to give him one last chance to escape. "Josh is a holy terror, and it's only going to get worse, Alex. The future holds cars and girls and s-e-x."

Alex flashed her a wolfish grin. "You're darn right I'm ready. Especially for the s-e-x."

"Alex, you can't talk that way in front of Josh!"

"You didn't hear that, did you, Josh?" he asked as he looked at the boy and winked.

"No," Josh answered. Then he rested his head on Alex's shoulder and said, "S-e-x."

"Joshua!" Erica exclaimed in horror.

Alex laughed, walked to her and wrapped his free arm around her. "Will you marry me?"

Erica looked up at him and nodded. "Yes, Alex. I'll marry you, but only under one condition."

He frowned. "What condition?"

She rubbed her hand on his stomach provocatively. "You have to promise me lots and lots of little Alexes. How else are we going to keep My Fair Baby as a satisfied client?"

She watched a series of emotions fly across his face. Surprise, uncertainty and vulnerability.

After a long, silent moment he drew in a deep breath and said, "Well, I might consider your condition if you'll consider mine."

"Which is?" Erica asked, grinning up at him.

"My Fair Baby has girl's clothes, too. I'll need at least one little Erica for every little Alex."

"I suppose we should keep the entire account in the family," she murmured as she raised on tiptoe and pressed a kiss to his lips, wondering if it was sinful to be this happy. She had a son she adored, a man she adored and a future that was filled with bright promise. What more could a woman possibly ask for?

PASSPORT TO ROMANCE VACATION SWEEPSTAKES

OFFICIAL RULES

SWEEPSTAKES RULES AND REGULATIONS. NO PURCHASE NECESSARY.

HOW TO ENTER:

1. To enter, complete this official entry form and return with your invoice in the envelope provided, or print your name, address, telephone number and age on a plain piece of paper and mail to: Passport to Romance, P.O. Box #1397, Buffalo, N.Y. 14269-1397. No mechanically reproduced entries accepted.
2. All entries must be received by the Contest Closing Date, midnight, December 31, 1990 to be eligible.
3. Prizes: There will be ten (10) Grand Prizes awarded, each consisting of a choice of a trip for two people to: i) London, England (approximate retail value $5,050 U.S.); ii) England, Wales and Scotland (approximate retail value $6,400 U.S.); iii) Caribbean Cruise (approximate retail value $7,300 U.S.); iv) Hawaii (approximate retail value $ 9,550 U.S.); v) Greek Island Cruise in the Mediterranean (approximate retail value $12,250 U.S.); vi) France (approximate retail value $7,300 U.S.).
4. Any winner may choose to receive any trip or a cash alternative prize of $5,000.00 U.S. in lieu of the trip.
5. Odds of winning depend on number of entries received.
6. A random draw will be made by Nielsen Promotion Services, an independent judging organization on January 29, 1991, in Buffalo, N.Y., at 11:30 a.m. from all eligible entries received on or before the Contest Closing Date. Any Canadian entrants who are selected must correctly answer a time-limited, mathematical skill-testing question in order to win. Quebec residents may submit any litigation respecting the conduct and awarding of a prize in this contest to the Régie des loteries et courses du Quebec.
7. Full contest rules may be obtained by sending a stamped, self-addressed envelope to: "Passport to Romance Rules Request", P.O. Box 9998, Saint John, New Brunswick, E2L 4N4.
8. Payment of taxes other than air and hotel taxes is the sole responsibility of the winner.
9. Void where prohibited by law.

PASSPORT TO ROMANCE VACATION SWEEPSTAKES

OFFICIAL RULES

SWEEPSTAKES RULES AND REGULATIONS. NO PURCHASE NECESSARY.

HOW TO ENTER:

1. To enter, complete this official entry form and return with your invoice in the envelope provided, or print your name, address, telephone number and age on a plain piece of paper and mail to: Passport to Romance, P.O. Box #1397, Buffalo, N.Y. 14269-1397. No mechanically reproduced entries accepted.
2. All entries must be received by the Contest Closing Date, midnight, December 31, 1990 to be eligible.
3. Prizes: There will be ten (10) Grand Prizes awarded, each consisting of a choice of a trip for two people to: i) London, England (approximate retail value $5,050 U.S.); ii) England, Wales and Scotland (approximate retail value $6,400 U.S.); iii) Caribbean Cruise (approximate retail value $7,300 U.S.); iv) Hawaii (approximate retail value $ 9,550 U.S.); v) Greek Island Cruise in the Mediterranean (approximate retail value $12,250 U.S.); vi) France (approximate retail value $7,300 U.S.).
4. Any winner may choose to receive any trip or a cash alternative prize of $5,000.00 U.S. in lieu of the trip.
5. Odds of winning depend on number of entries received.
6. A random draw will be made by Nielsen Promotion Services, an independent judging organization on January 29, 1991, in Buffalo, N.Y., at 11:30 a.m. from all eligible entries received on or before the Contest Closing Date. Any Canadian entrants who are selected must correctly answer a time-limited, mathematical skill-testing question in order to win. Quebec residents may submit any litigation respecting the conduct and awarding of a prize in this contest to the Régie des loteries et courses du Quebec.
7. Full contest rules may be obtained by sending a stamped, self-addressed envelope to: "Passport to Romance Rules Request", P.O. Box 9998, Saint John, New Brunswick, E2L 4N4.
8. Payment of taxes other than air and hotel taxes is the sole responsibility of the winner
9. Void where prohibited by law.

 RLS-DIR

PASSPORT TO ROMANCE
WIN 1 of 10 Vacations
SEE INSIDE

VACATION SWEEPSTAKES

MONTH 2 ENTRY

Official Entry Form

Yes, enter me in the drawing for one of ten Vacations-for-Two! If I'm a winner, I'll get my choice of any of the six different destinations being offered — and I won't have to decide until after I'm notified!

Return entries with invoice in envelope provided along with Daily Travel Allowance Voucher. Each book in your shipment has two entry forms — and the more you enter, the better your chance of winning!

Name ______________________________

Address ______________________________ Apt. ______

City ______________ State/Prov. ______________ Zip/Postal Code ______________

Daytime phone number ______________________________
Area Code

☐ I am enclosing a Daily Travel Allowance Voucher in the amount of $__________ Write in amount revealed beneath scratch-off

PASSPORT TO ROMANCE
WIN 1 of 10 Vacations
SEE INSIDE

VACATION SWEEPSTAKES

MONTH 2 ENTRY

Official Entry Form

Yes, enter me in the drawing for one of ten Vacations-for-Two! If I'm a winner, I'll get my choice of any of the six different destinations being offered — and I won't have to decide until after I'm notified!

Return entries with invoice in envelope provided along with Daily Travel Allowance Voucher. Each book in your shipment has two entry forms — and the more you enter, the better your chance of winning!

Name ______________________________

Address ______________________________ Apt. ______

City ______________ State/Prov. ______________ Zip/Postal Code ______________

Daytime phone number ______________________________
Area Code

☐ I am enclosing a Daily Travel Allowance Voucher in the amount of $__________ Write in amount revealed beneath scratch-off

CPS-TWO